Tr

By I

This is a story of a wondrous journey of which I am honored to have had the pleasure of bringing to you. It is a privilege to have worked with a truly gifted editor with the unique ability to bring this story to you.

Thank You for all the great places and great times that I have had the pleasure of sharing to make this story possible. This story is the beginnings of a far larger journey I hope everyone enjoys.

This is a work of fiction. Names, characters, places, and incidents either are the product of the author's imagination or are used fictitiously. Any resemblance to actual persons, living or dead, events, or locales is entirely coincidental.

Special Thanks to For Goodness Sakes Productions and the inspiring movie of Everglades of the North Production

ISBN# 978-0-9894697-1-5

Dennis [illegible]

[illegible]

Table of Contents

Chapter 1 Elisabeth

One fine time ago, the whispering creak of the old screen door draws Ida's attention to the pure, little girl entering her home.

"Grandma, we're here!" Elisabeth calls.

"I'm in the parlor, dear," Ida says.

Elisabeth runs around the foyer, past the plants, and into the parlor, beaming from ear to ear. "Look what I got, Grandma!" She holds out her hand to show Ida a gleaming, medallion sized coin.

"Oh! Let me see what you have there." Ida's feeble hands reach out, and showing their past strength she grasps the heavy, golden coin. "What is it, my dear?"

"It's a geocoin Mom got for me. People hide them all over the world for others to find."

"Oh, we are holding it, are people finding us right now?" Ida asks.

"No, Mom," says Elisabeth's mom, Trinity. "It's a coin you can hide anywhere and people look for it. It's sort of a game to learn how to find things on a map. You can go on the Internet and use this geocaching website to locate items in hidden places.

Then you can write about what you found. It's Elisabeth's new hobby. I was reading on the website that it teaches kids about spatial science. That means how to read a map. Elisabeth is learning how to use digital maps on her computer, and how to use the geocaching app on her cell phone."

"Oh, I see. It sounds a little confusing," Ida says.

"Yeah, Grandma. Yesterday we used my cell to find a hidden cache. It wasn't easy either."

"What's a cache, dear?" Ida says.

"Grandma, it's a container holding different things for people to find and trade. The person who finds it can move the things inside it to a different cache."

"That sounds nice to go out on a treasure hunt and find things. A treasure hunt is always fun," Ida says.

"So, Mom, we came over to see how you were. Elisabeth keeps pestering me to come over especially after she found this geo thing on the Internet and got that coin to show you," says Trinity.

"Oh, I have been just fine keeping busy around the house. You know, over the years, I have accumulated so much stuff I need to go through it all to see what I should keep and what to get rid of," Ida says.

"Yeah, Mom, you have had a great life, almost magical in a sense. When I was growing up it seemed like everything always worked out for us. We never worried about finances. You remember the time our car went kaput and Dad needed to replace it quickly because his new job started the next Monday? You were looking through your purse for the mechanic's number and you found a note from Grandpa that said to make sure to check the safety deposit box after his effects were settled. We went down to the bank that Friday and opened the box to find enough money to buy a brand new car," Trinity says.

"Well dear, I never wanted to admit it, but I have always recognized the way things worked out for us financially. Seems in the toughest times a way always opened up to get through. It never opened up enough to leap too far ahead, but just enough for things to work out ok for us," Ida says.

"Grandma, I think there is a geocache close to your house. Can we go look for it?" asks

Elisabeth. “Can we go, Mom? Please? Please?” Elisabeth asks Trinity.

“Well, I don’t know. If Grandma is up to it, I guess we can go. Let me see how far away it is.”

“Oh dear, I would really like to go. It’s nice out and Elisabeth wants to show me, too,” Ida says.

“Ok then, let’s go,” Trinity says with a smile.

As Ida gets ready, Elisabeth is already out the front door and at the end of the sidewalk.

“This way, Grandma, it’s not too far, just a couple of blocks around the corner.”

As they try to slow Elisabeth down and make their way to the cache, Ida recalls some of her earlier days of being outdoors in the country and living on the farm. Those were good days and filled with such wonderful experiences. She vividly remembers the smell of the open air and the quiet times near the river. The serenity was far better than the distraction the city had become in the last few years. Her city was growing and changing at such a quick pace. Ida remembers the way it was when she first moved into town. It was busy, but not as intense as it is today. It seems people's patience gets shorter each year. People want and need results and have trouble waiting any amount of time to get them.

"Grandma, right here is where it should be. Right here somewhere. My phone app says 'it's hidden on a device of the past, so be discreet, and see if you can find it'," Elisabeth reads.

"Your phone says all that?" Ida asks. Oh, the times change so fast, she thinks to herself. "That is so neat that your phone shows you where it is and then gives clues to find it. Let's see if we can find it, Elisabeth."

They look all over, but the intersection doesn't seem to want to give up its find so easily.

"Well, let's see," says Trinity. "What would be a device from the past?"

Ida looks around and says "I don't see anything out of the ordinary here. The stoplight is just like when I moved here. The old store front may be closed, but it hasn't changed either."

"But Grandma, what's that?" Elisabeth asks and points to something across the street.

"Where, dear?" asks Ida as she hurries over to Elisabeth's side.

"Over there. Why would there be a phone that takes money next to that building? Everyone has a cell phone now. Why would anyone pay to use an old phone without a screen on it?" asks Elisabeth.

"Hey! That's it! You found it, Elisabeth! It's by the public pay phone!" says Trinity.

"Oh yes, you are right," Ida says. "I would have looked right past it. It is not so long ago that we all needed those phones. Let's look to see if anything is out of place."

"Here it is! I found it!" Elisabeth says. "It's right there on the back!"

There it is. A magnetic key holder stuck to the back of the pay phone pedestal.

"I will get it," says Trinity. With a small tug the magnet releases from the pedestal and Trinity has it in her hand.

"Oh, too cool," says Elisabeth. "Let's open it up and see what's in there."

"Yes, that is really neat. I have been by that phone hundreds of times and would never have thought to look for anything like that. What's in it?" asks Ida.

As Trinity opens the magnetic holder, a scroll of paper, a pen, and a playing card fall out.

"What do we do now?" Ida asks Elisabeth.

"Well, don't be silly, Grandma. First, we write our names in the log. See, it's the paper scroll. Then we trade something in the cache, like that card, with something we already have. Then we can move that card we took to another spot. That's the way the game is played."

"Well, that sounds really swell. How about you sign it, Elisabeth?" Ida says.

"Remember to put the date on it," says Trinity.

"We will put it all back together and leave it where we found it then, right?" asks Ida.

"Yes, Mom, that's how it works. Then someone else can find it after us. We will log in to our online geocaching account to say we found it and that we traded something. We leave this information to help the next person," explains Trinity. "But, we can do that later, Elisabeth, because we need to get going to finish our errands today. Grandma doesn't have a computer or Internet, so we will have to wait until we get home."

"Ok, Mom," agrees Elisabeth. "Maybe we can get Grandma a computer with her very own geocaching account so she can play, too, and we can watch each other's geocaching finds."

"We will have to look into that," says Ida. "I may need to get up to speed after all so I can keep up with my granddaughter." Ida gives Trinity a wink.

Trinity gives her mom a quizzical look thinking Ida is just amusing Elisabeth. They make their way back to Ida's house and say goodbye for the day.

"That sure was fun, Elisabeth. I hope we do this again real soon. Next time let's go a little farther," says Ida.

"Ok, Grandma." Elisabeth says as she beams from ear to ear. I have the coolest Grandma, ever, she thinks to herself.

Chapter 2 Grandma Ida

"Hello, Mom. I was just calling to see what time the telephone guy was coming," Trinity asks Ida.

"Well, he should be here anytime now. They told me to make room for something called a modem."

"Alright, I'm on my way."

Ida hangs up the phone and rushes to the sitting room, as fast as her weary body can take her. She remembers when she could shoot across a room in no time, but these days she has to steady herself along the way.

She has just enough time to try to move the bureau to make room for the modem. She wonders to herself whether there is enough space. She struggles to move the bureau away from the telephone jack, but is determined to do this by herself. With a final shove, she succeeds.

"Mom, I'm here, where are you?" Trinity calls.

"I am in the sitting room, making space for the modem."

"Mom, why are you doing that? You should have waited until I got here! A modem is not that big. It's small enough to fit on top of your desk."

"Oh, dear, how should I know? In my day, electric things were so large I figured I would need to make room."

"Well, you will be amazed, Mom."

The doorbell rings. Trinity looks out the window to see the telephone company's truck and opens the door.

"Good Morning Ladies. I'm Stan. I'm here to install your Internet service. What room would you like to put your modem?"

"In here, by this desk. My stubborn mother moved this to the side to make enough room," Trinity says.

"Why, that will certainly be plenty of room," Stan says and grins. "I will need to go outside and check the telephone box for data."

"Mom, how many phones do you have in the house now?" asks Trinity.

"I only have two, one in the bedroom, and one in the living room. The one I had in the kitchen quit on me so I took it to church when they had their recycling day."

"Good idea. You should try to get a cordless phone so you can take it with you wherever you are in the house."

"Please, Trinity, one thing at a time, and maybe after I learn how to use this Internet thing."

Stan returns from outside. "I have everything ready on the outside of the house, so now I need to plug in the modem and check your connection. Can you show me where your other phones are so I can plug these filters in so the data will not interrupt your voice phone line? I have three on me and more in the truck."

Stan plugs the modem into the wall jack and places it on the desk. He plugs the phone into the other splitter jack with the voice filter.

"My word, that thing really is small," Ida says. "That can fit right into the top envelope slot in my desk."

"Yes, that would be fine, but it does need some air around it to keep it cool. Try not to stack things around it," replies Stan.

Stan plugs in the filters, and checks all the phones. His last step is to check the data link on the modem to make sure there is throughput. As he works, he explains to Trinity and Ida what throughput means.

"It's data coming through at a certain speed to help your internet access run smoothly," Stan says. He sets up the modem and powers it up. As the lights turn on, he connects his data analyzer to the output port. It lights up and his screen registers a number. "Well it's looking good. Think you're ready to hook up your computer now."

"My mom hasn't got her computer yet, she wanted to make sure she could get the Internet first before she spends the money," Trinity says.

Stan gathers his equipment and heads for the door. "If you need help with your computer, give us a call. I'm impressed that you are getting the Internet at your age. I guess it's never too late."

Ida and Trinity thank Stan. As Ida closes the door, she thinks about what Stan said about throughput. It sounds similar to what the pastor was talking about in last Sunday's sermon. He talked about how important it was to "pay it forward". Ida was pretty sure she understood what that meant, and it seemed to her that throughput was another good way to describe it.

Trinity says goodbye and assures Ida that she and Elisabeth would see her Thursday to go buy the computer and help her set it up. Ida thanks her daughter with a hug and tells her to give one to Elisabeth, too.

Thursday comes rather quickly. Ida is sitting in her knitting chair and looks out to see Trinity and Elisabeth pull in the driveway. Eager to go, she gets up, grabs her shawl and purse, and heads to the car. On Trinity's suggestion, they go to the office supply store.

"I brought the store flyer along," Ida says. Elisabeth browses the flyer, points to the best deal, and Ida agrees. The store is not too busy and they are soon out the door.

"I think you picked a good one, Grandma," Elisabeth says.

"Oh, yes, dear, I am really excited to see this Internet thing!"

"Grandma, you are too funny."

Soon they return to Ida's house. Trinity carries the computer and Elisabeth helps Ida out of the car. It has been a tiring day for Ida.

"Right there, dear, on the desk, will be fine," Ida says.

"Ok, Grandma, I will have it set up in a few minutes."

"Would you like some lemonade while you work, Elisabeth?" Ida asks.

"I will get it," Trinity says and heads for the kitchen. "You just sit down and relax for a bit, you've had a long day."

Elisabeth sets up the computer. The cooling fan whirs to life and it boots up. "That is the program sound, Grandma. It will make that sound each time you turn it on." The computer loads up. Elisabeth runs through the set up and logs in to the Internet modem data link. "It's online now. You're on the Internet!"

"Oh, that was so fast, dear, I'm on the Internet? Well aren't I a mover and a shaker now?" Ida says.

"You need an email address, so I will go to yahoo and make one."

"I already have a mail address. You know it's on my front door."

"You are so silly, Grandma. It's an email address, not a house address. We need a name and a password. Hmm, how about grandmaida35@yahoo.com?"

Elisabeth whispers the password to Ida. "Oh, I had better write all that down," Ida says. She quickly finds a pen and puts the note in a hidden place in her desk. Then she remembers to ask Elisabeth about the "geo world thing" they were doing the other day.

"It's called 'geocaching' and they have a website. I will go to the site and set up a username for you so we can share our finds," Elisabeth says. "It's free, so don't worry about paying and if anyone ever asks you to pay for something or asks you for any information, always say no. There are people on the Internet who are always trying to get information to do bad things."

"You mean like the people always calling me on the phone trying to sell things?"

"Yes, just like that."

Trinity brings in three cold glasses of lemonade as Elisabeth finishes up with the computer.

"You're all set up now, Grandma."

Ida smiles and thanks Elisabeth with the strongest hug her old, tired arms can give.

Chapter 3 Geocaching

Ida gets up early because she and Elisabeth have a big day planned together. Ida looks out the window as she drinks her hot coffee. It looks chilly, and somewhat cloudy. She goes to put on a sweater and sits down at the computer. After a few minutes, she hears the front door.

"Come in, dear. Thank heavens you're here! I was trying to look at this geo thing all by myself to see what we could do today," Ida says.

"Let me help. I see you got logged in all by yourself! That's cool," says Elisabeth.

"Yes, I am proud I got that much done."

"Let's see where you are. Looks like we need to go to the map," Elisabeth says and she shows Ida how to get to the map and zoom in to some cache points.

"Oh, swell. How about this one? It's just outside town and looks like a whole string of items to find," says Ida.

"Let's do that. I think that's called a series when they're all bunched together like that."

"How about we get our things, and get in the car," Ida says.

Ida drives at her usual snail's pace, so it gives Elisabeth plenty of time to log into her phone app and get a plan together. They drive out of town and head south.

"We are getting close to the first one, Grandma, it should be just ahead. We must keep our eyes open to see where the most likely place would be."

"There is a large, old tree there, dear, but I don't see much else except picked corn fields."

"Good eye! That might be it. Pull over and I will get out and look around. The description says it's a place that took decades to come about. That sounds like a clue that it could be that tree," Elisabeth says and puts her gloves and hat on.

Ida turns her hazard lights on, and pulls off to the side of the country road. She usually worries about passing cars, but thankfully, this road seems pretty quiet. Elisabeth gets out and walks around the tree several times. She looks high and low, to no avail.

“How’s it going?” calls Ida from inside the car. It’s a chilly, windy day, and Ida doesn’t feel up to braving the cold.

“It’s not. I don’t see anything except bark and leaves.” Discouraged, Elisabeth looks at her phone again and rereads the clues and posts made by people who have already been there. She shows these to Ida, who can’t believe she is reading all of this on a phone.

Elisabeth reads some more. “This one says ‘an easy find, a grab and go’ and this one says ‘look low and dark, it’s small but not hard to find’.” Determined not to give up, she decides to look in the opening she finds at the bottom of the tree trunk. It’s the only place she thinks it could be. Ida hollers to her to be careful, since there is poison ivy growing around the opening. Elisabeth so very carefully reaches inside.

“Oh, my gosh! Here it is! I found it!”

“You did? Open it up!” says Ida. This is more fun than she ever thought it would be, she thinks to herself.

Elisabeth unscrews the top of the small bottle to find a pen, a paper log, and a toy race car. They sign their names in the log with the pen and are sure to put the date, too, so others would know they found it. Ida digs through her coat pocket and pulls out an old, silver penny. She hands it to Elisabeth who places it in the cache bottle. Then Elisabeth rolls up the paper log, puts the pen and the toy car back, and screws the top back on tightly. She makes sure the top is on good and tight so it doesn't get wet inside the bottle.

"I will put it back right where I found it," Elisabeth says. Ida watches the road for cars while Elisabeth returns the cache to its resting place in the opening of the old tree trunk.

"Well, that sure was neat. Can we go to another one?" asks Ida.

"Yeah, there is another about a mile down the road. The map says this is a series with a theme and they're all put out by the same person." So, Ida and Elisabeth continue their drive to the next one, while Elisabeth watches the map on her phone. She has the GPS turned on so it shows her where they are and how far they are from the next cache.

"Here's the spot, Grandma, but I don't see a tree. The only thing here is that guardrail." Elisabeth keeps reading the clues from the geocaching app. The first clue says it's small and clings tightly to its place.

“Maybe it’s another magnet, like the one on the pay phone,” Ida says.

Agreeing that would make sense, Elisabeth gets out and searches around the guardrail. After a minute or two, her small hands manage to locate something her eyes can’t see. Indeed, it is a small, magnetized geocache box stuck inside the guardrail. What a very clever hiding place, Ida thought. They sign the log, and leave another old, silver penny that Ida has. They put the cache back in its place and go on to look for the rest in the series.

After finding nine out of ten, Ida says they need to head back before it gets dark. She is feeling very tired, and not fond of driving around at night. Before she leaves Ida’s house, Elisabeth shows Ida how to log their visits on the computer for each cache they found. They make a plan to do this again on Saturday.

Chapter 4 Lomax Station

Saturday comes around. The day warms up nicely after a cool, dew filled morning. Ida sees Trinity's car pull up and Elisabeth jumps out. She waves goodbye to her mom and runs up to the front door. She finds her Grandma Ida in front of the computer. Ida has logged in to her geocaching account the way Elisabeth showed her, but she is having trouble understanding the map. "Dear, I need help seeing the places we went to," Ida says.

"You need to zoom in a little. You have it set to see the whole world at once," Elisabeth points out. The map is filled with so many dots that it looks like one big dot.

"There are really that many caches around the world?" Ida asks. She thinks to herself how adventurous it would be to go looking for them all. For an instant she wishes she was young again.

"Yes, there are enough around to keep us busy for a while." Elisabeth shows her how to zoom in and out and navigate around the map. They go to the area they visited last Saturday. "Wow, look here, there have been people there after us, already. They have logged their visit." Elisabeth shows Ida how to click on each tag to read everything about the cache.

"Now, everyone will see where we've been," Ida says. "This is just like leaving a message in a bottle!"

Elisabeth looks up at Ida. "What's a message in a bottle?"

Ida sits back in her chair and gives Elisabeth a long, thoughtful look. "Well, dear, I keep forgetting how young you really are. You seem so mature for your age. Let me try to explain. A message in a bottle is a long tradition, with a lot of romance. It's a long shot at connecting with strangers. It's a chance connection born from pure karma. Someone would take a bottle and put a message in it and let it float away in the water. Sometimes people put them in the ocean, sometimes in a river. Then they waited. If they were lucky, someone would find the bottle and read the message and try to find the person who sent it."

Elisabeth's mouth drops open and the look on her face says she can't believe what her Grandma is telling her. "But the chances of that little bottle ever getting anywhere and into someone's hands are very small," Elisabeth says.

"Still, it is such a romantic notion to think somebody would find your message and come to look for you. Believe it or not, there were days when there were no phones. If there was mail, it took a long time to get to where it needed to go. That is what makes the message in a bottle so neat. It is a chance in a million," Ida says.

"Wow, yeah, now we just text each other when we want to talk. There's no waiting for that," Elisabeth says.

"And there is no anticipation, and that is sometimes the best part," Ida replies.

Ida continues to tell Elisabeth more stories. "When I was growing up, dear, we lived down by the river. I would go out there every day after school. It was so quiet and peaceful. The river would just flow by and you could hear the animals in the distance."

"Mom told me you had a tough struggle when you were younger."

"No, it was not that tough. It was filled with nature every moment. I really enjoyed it looking back now. You know, Elisabeth, I see you are growing up fast. Someday you will look back at these days with fond memories and see what a good time it was. I am so happy you spend time with your old grandma. I know you could be out with your friends instead of listening to my boring, old stories."

"Oh, no, I always have fun with you. When I do go out with my friends, I tell them all about you and your adventures. They can't believe all the things you have done. I love to hear your stories, so please tell me some more," Elisabeth pleads.

Ida searches her memory for a story to tell Elisabeth, but is distracted by the sound coming from the television. It's the tornado scene from the movie "The Wizard of Oz".

Elisabeth jumps up and runs to the television. "I love this movie! Can we watch it?"

The two of them snuggle up on the couch as the movie plays. Watching the movie triggers Ida's memory, so she begins to tell the tale that she was once told. The story goes that there is a road down by the Yellow River called Toto Road. That was how Toto, the dog, got his name. They say, Frank Baum, the man who wrote the book the "Wizard of Oz", would spend his summers in the area. The locals like to believe that place inspired his writings.

"Can we go there?" asks Elisabeth.

"Well, yes, dear, we will go there. Maybe we will find out who the Wizard of Oz really is?" Ida laughs and her mind starts to race. She continues on with another tale.

"Well, you see the Yellow River flows to the west into the Kankakee River. Then the Kankakee flows to the Mississippi River and into the Gulf of Mexico," Ida begins. Elisabeth leans forward in interest, so Ida continues. "I would sit down by the river and think of all the travels it was getting ready for as it flowed by. Our ancestors moved here from out East, as far as I know. I think it was my great grandfather who came to the English Lake area when he was a young man. They called it that because it was a very large lake back then. It was filled with all sorts of wildlife. It was truly a glorious paradise in its day. He came here to a small railroad town call Lomax Station. It was near a place where they used to pump oil to Chicago. There was this oil, called skunk oil, named so because when they burned it, it smelled like a skunk. But, there was a possibility to make a fortune if they could refine it to get rid of the smell. That's why he went there, to lend his help in finding a way. He had a little bit of money because he seemed to do well with his investments. You see, oil was the big thing back then, because it was powering everything."

“So, he was going to make a lot of money?” Elisabeth asks.

“Yes, dear, that was his plan,” says Ida.

Ida closes her eyes and pauses for a second to gather her thoughts. The pictures in her mind change from color to black and white, and she tells Elisabeth the story.

He came here on the railroad. It was a cold spring morning when the train pulled into the station. There were only a few people getting off at Lomax. When he got off the train, he needed to find his way to the pumping station. There was a farm house nearby, with a farmer there who knew how to get to the pumping station, so he gave him directions. He was so thankful that he bought a horse from the farmer. He loaded his luggage onto the horse and rode north along the wagon trail. It wasn’t too far. When he got there he saw a group of people hustling and bustling about between a rather large building and a smaller one.

The sun rose higher in the sky and the fog burned off to reveal a crystal clear day. The sun was beaming the warmth he needed and he felt rejuvenated. There were people working all around the site. He went up to a guy holding a large steel beam and asked who the person in charge was. The man said “that would be Joshua and he is over in the telegraph house. It’s the small building between the sleeping quarters and this big one right here”. As he walks, he notices smoke billowing heavily out of the enormously tall smokestack and tracing south across the sky.

As he makes his way into the office, he is greeted by three people. One is taking notes while another taps out a message on the telegraph. Another person is sitting behind a desk looking over some schedules, so he addresses him.

“I presume you are Joshua,” the newcomer asks.

“Yes, I am Joshua. I presume you are Simon. You came a long way, but we are grateful you’re here. This whole operation is going well, but we need to find the right refining solution to make all this skunk oil usable.”

“Well, I thought you already had. I was starting to wonder what I was doing here. It doesn’t smell bad. You are using it, aren’t you?” asks Simon.

“Yes, yes we are. It doesn’t smell bad because you see that unbelievably tall chimney? It was not made that tall for looks. It is the only way we can keep this operation going until we find the right mixture or else it would smell something awful around here," Joshua says.

"I was wondering why that chimney is three times bigger than any I have seen in such a remote place."

Joshua rose from his chair and stepped around his large oak desk. "Let me take you around to show you how things work around here, then you can tell me how you can help us. First, let's get you a place for your things." Joshua leads Simon to the bunk building where he puts his things in a locked chest by an open bunk.

"Thank you, Joshua, this should do fine. It's a lot better than that seat on the train."

As Simon puts his things away, Joshua gets out a group of folded papers and shuffles to a worn page that is dirty and creased on the corners. "I need to show you this," Joshua says. "It's a process design to separate the organics from the oil that would refine the skunk oil into something usable on the whole commodity market. This is the last try we received from the Chicago office because they were at an impasse for a solution. They have tried every known method to separate the negative organics from the oil to leave a usable product.

Simon, I heard you have studied under a renowned chemist in your early education days out East."

"Yes, I have, and he was a truly brilliant chemist. He possessed the ability to step back and look at things in hindsight. In doing so, it seemed to show him something that was there the whole time, but had been over looked because it was the simplest solution," Simon explains.

"Please, take a look at these findings and see if anything looks out of place to you. We desperately need to find a solution because even though the owners, the Rockefellers, have an immense fortune, they cannot continue down this path of buying skunk oil and shipping it to the refining facility without having an effective refining technique in place."

Joshua handed the worn papers to Simon to look over. "The basic premise looks good. A separation technique is the most logical." Simon was about to continue his comment when a burly man rushed in.

"Joshua! We need you to come quick! The main flywheel has shifted! It's going to scar the bearing and that will lock up the whole pump station piston!"

They all run over to the large building. Inside Simon sees a 20 foot tall wheel with a belt around it. The wheel is halfway in the ground and the belt stretches out to the pump shed to the west.

Joshua sees the situation is grim. "Whoa! It's going to seize up! We need to get the push bar over on the pivot bearing and force it back into the saddle. I need three guys now! Hold this, Simon, and make sure you don't lose those papers. They are critical to this operation." Simon grabs the papers and tucks them safely into his pocket. The men struggle with the pry bar shaft until finally the wheel pivots onto the saddle.

Nervously wiping the sweat from his brow, Joshua commends his men for a job well done. "Now get that bearing greased. Tighten the saddle, and score the bolt to keep it from rocking loose. We have to keep that pulley running to maintain the line pressure for the product to transfer." The men take their orders from Joshua and hurry off.

As they walk back to the telegraph office, Simon pulls the papers out of his pocket. A leather pouch falls out. "You've dropped something, Simon," Joshua says.

"Oh, thank you. I can't lose that, it's an old family heirloom that has been in my family longer than anyone can remember," Simon replies gratefully.

Joshua's curiosity is peaked so he takes a glance at the pouch. "It does look old, but in great condition for its age." He notices some dust leaking from the corner. "What kind of dust is that?" he asks Simon.

"I'm not sure, but I've seen it fall out of the pouch before. I would really like to know myself," Simon replies.

"Let's take it over to the lab and see what they think it is," Joshua suggests. Simon agrees and the two men make their way to the lab. Inside are a couple of scientists surrounded by various containers of the black oil.

"Hello, men, this is Simon. He has this gray dust he can't identify so I am asking for your help to see what it is." The men move closer to examine the pouch.

One man says it looks like a highly metallic lime dust. He tells them that he has seen something like it out in a wet area of the stone quarry. He says it's very abundant and is usually piled up to mix as filler later for different uses. Its metallic composition tends to make it less desirable. The other man asks Simon to bring the sample over to his table. He takes a flask of the dreaded skunk oil and goes to get the separator equipment.

"You know we have tried that a thousand times," says his assistant.

"I know, but not with this particular metallic in the limestone dust," the scientist replies. The men run the separator and place a bit of the metallic dust inside. The process divides the mixture into two products: a clear formula and the normal black oil. The assistant takes the black oil that is left after the byproduct is removed and puts it into the lamp on his table.

"Oh, no, this is going to be bad," Joshua says and he pinches his nose closed.

"We will see," the scientist says, "we will see."

"Hold your nose, Simon, I have been here too many times to know this is going to be bad," Joshua tells Simon.

All of the men hold their breath. They ignite the oil product, and it flames up quickly, and turns a bright yellow. "Well, that is mighty, mighty interesting," the assistant says.

"I have never seen you get it to light that quickly before!" Joshua says scratching his head in disbelief.

"What's the problem? I think it puts off a nice, steady glow. It doesn't even have a bad odor," observes Simon.

"No, it doesn't. Say, are you guys fooling me? Did you switch the oils? That can't be the skunk oil we are pumping!" Joshua says dumbfounded.

"Yes, yes it is the skunk oil," both men say in unison.

They all stand there, in awe, and watch the oil burn. They can't believe their own eyes. For a few moments, all that can be heard is the breeze rustling through the leaves outside. Joshua breaks the silence. "I think we have something here. Let's get this process telegraphed to Chicago to see if they obtain the same result." The others agree. Joshua turns to Simon and says "This is a miracle. The solution was simply here the whole time. How did you know? How can we ever thank you enough?"

“Oh, it was nothing. I’m just glad I could be of help to you, Joshua,” and Simon gives him a sly grin.

Joshua and Simon rush over to the telegraph building and tap out the solution to headquarters. It will be a long wait until they hear back on the results. Joshua tells Simon it’s getting toward dusk, so he might want to get to the bunk house before the mosquitos carry him away. Simon agrees and says goodnight.

The next morning breaks without a fog or haze. Simon awakes and goes to see Joshua. Joshua hasn’t heard back from headquarters yet, and everything else is quiet and running smooth. Joshua asks Simon if he would like to go for a ride up the river so he can show him the joys of being down here beside the daily toll of the oil pumping life. Simon excitedly agrees and they walk down to the river and get in a small canoe. They push off and head north upstream, so that when they tire, they can float back down to the pumping station.

They paddle up the river without much difficulty. The current is flowing gently against them and the trip goes smoothly. Joshua turns to Simon and points to something in the distance. “Up here is one of the older homesteads on the river. I don’t know how old exactly, but as long as anyone can remember, that family has lived there.”

As they paddle past the house, they see the family out doing chores. They exchange a friendly wave as they pass by. Simon is struck immediately by the young lady who is hanging out the laundry. Her glow in front of the morning sun is indescribable.

“Who is she?” Simon asks Joshua.

“Well, she is Adelaide. She comes to the pumping station once in a while to give us special desserts of cakes and cookies. When she comes down, I will introduce you to her.”

“Oh please do. I must meet her,” Simon replies.

They paddle upstream until they get to the large river that intersects with the Kankakee. Joshua suggests that this is the perfect spot to turn back. The area is a great hunting and fishing lake and they need to be careful. It is full of hunters and sometimes shots go astray. Simon agrees wholeheartedly knowing he hopes to see Adelaide again on the way back.

As they float southerly and with the current, they pass the old homestead. Simon is dismayed that he sees no one is outside, so they continue on their way back to the pumping station and dock the canoe.

"Any word from headquarters, yet?" Joshua asks the foreman at the telegraph.

"No, no word yet, just the normal news and sports scores," the foreman replies.

Simon turns to Joshua and asks if he won the bet. Joshua looks quizzically at Simon, and wonders how he knew he bet on sports. "Why, no, I lost," says Joshua.

"You keep betting on the Chicago teams. You may be the biggest fan, but you lose the bet every time," Simon laughs.

"That's ok. They will pull through sometime," Joshua replies and scratches his head in wonder.

As they walk over to the pump house, Simon stops silent in his pace. There she is, Adelaide, with the setting sun all around her.

Joshua turns and sees what has grabbed Simon's attention. "Adelaide! I'm so glad you came. I just want some of your delicious cake, but I also need to introduce you to Simon. He is from out

East, and stopped here on his way to Chicago," Joshua says.

"Pleased to meet you, Adelaide," Simon manages.

"Pleased to meet you, Simon," Adelaide replies as she blushes.

"The pleasure is all mine."

Joshua excuses himself, bids the two good evening, and makes his way to his office. Simon and Adelaide walk along the path and talk. "I hope you don't think I'm being too forward, but how about a sunset walk to the river?" Simon asks. "I would be honored to hear some stories of the area."

"Oh, why yes, I could oblige you," says Adelaide.

The two walk down to the river's sandy bank. They sit in the warm sand along the water's edge, and converse until the dusk sets in. Adelaide needs to head back home.

"It's getting dark, let me grab a lantern, and walk you home," says Simon.

"Oh, you would do that for me?" Adelaide says.

"Yes, I would be honored."

The walk to Adelaide's house is magical, and the quiet night air is intoxicating. Simon wishes her a good night and walks back to the pumping station. He is halfway there when he suddenly hears clanging and loud gunshots off in the distance.

That sounds like trouble, he thinks to himself, so he starts into a full sprint back to the station. When he gets there, he sees a group of men running towards the pump house and he wonders what happened. He sees Joshua, who looks very dismayed.

"I was walking back and heard a lot of commotion. What's going on?" Simon asks Joshua.

"They hit us! They hit us!" Joshua says and drops his head into his hands. "There's a band of horse thieves that come around once in a blue moon. They stole a few of our horses. It looks like they headed west. They took your horse too, Simon," Joshua laments.

"Who are they?" asks Simon.

"Well, lore has it, they hang out at a place southwest of here they call Bogus Island. It's in the middle of a swamp called Beaver Lake. Many men have gone out after them, but to my knowledge, none made it back. We need to be more vigilant next time and take care of them once and for all if they come around again. They are a wily bunch, so you have to know their territory better than they think you do."

The next day, Simon helps the crew keep the pumping station running smoothly. He spends the most time he can with Adelaide.

On Friday, some of the workers are heading north to a town called LaCrosse. They need to get some supplies and take a break from the long week. Simon has heard interesting stories of the times they have had there, so he goes along to see for himself.

The room is quiet, except for the television, when Ida opens her eyes. She and Elisabeth are still on the couch. Elisabeth is staring at her.

"None of my friends are going to believe that one, Grandma," Elisabeth mutters.

"Well, you haven't heard anything yet, Elisabeth," Ida replies, and continues on.

Chapter 5 Bogus Island

The ride to LaCrosse is short. As Simon rides to what seems like a small intersection of old wagon trails, he is amazed at the multitude of people he sees. There are people everywhere and the buildings are bustling with crowds. There is band music echoing throughout the plain.

"Come on over!" the workers shout. "Simon! Over here!" They lead him to a small building that looks like a saloon. "This is where you want to be!" they say. "It's only like this a few times a year, so have a good time."

Simon strides up to the bar and orders a whiskey. "Stronger than anything you have ever had," says the bartender.

"Oh, you would be surprised. I just got in from the East coast, so I'll see about that." Simon eyes the glass and gulps the shot down. He begins to cough. "Whoa, that has a kick!" he says.

"Yes sir, that's from Shorty's still. It's pretty strong stuff," says a local as he pats Simon on the back. "You ok there, Mister?"

"Yes, thank you, I will be fine."

The stranger offers a handshake to Simon. “My name is Jenks. I see you can handle the strong stuff. Not many try and fewer can stomach it. Some friends of mine over there are playing a little poker. You want in?” Jenks asks.

Simon takes a glance at the poker table. “Well, sure, sounds fun if you folks like losing money.”

“Then come on over here. Let’s see how fast we like losing money,” Jenks snorts.

Jenks leads Simon over to the table. The players look quite rough with not the best histories. “Look here, boys, we have ourselves an Easterner who says we should be scared of losing money!” Jenks says. The men laugh out loud and pull up a chair for Simon.

“Deal me in,” says Simon and he orders a round of drinks.

The card playing goes on into the early morning and the liquor is flowing freely. Simon wins some and loses some. During the game, Jenks and his men talk about the trouble they get into. They tell Simon they are only in town to have some fun and spend some of their ill begotten gains.

Simon is quite intrigued, so he coaxes them into telling their tales.

Jenks pipes in, "We make money fast and lots of it, especially from the East Coasters." They all laugh. "They love our fast horses and never ask about where we got them. We can get you the best horse and you can make a quick dollar, too."

As the night turns into dawn, Jenks takes a great liking to Simon. He tells Simon to meet him and his men in two days, fifteen miles west of here, at the hunting lodge near the swamps.

"You will know it when you see it," Jenks assures Simon. Simon agrees to it and heads back to Lomax Station to rest up.

In two days' time, as planned, Simon borrows a company horse and heads toward the west. He finds the swamp just as he was told. Suddenly, Jenks comes up from behind.

"I didn't think you would come out here. We are just pulling out now. Follow us to the island. The boys want to take some more of your money," Jenks laughs.

They travel west and it seems the terrain only gets worse. Simon grows more and more concerned with each step as they ride further and further into what seems like an endless swamp. Suddenly, the foliage breaks open and a large lake appears. It looks like its receding because its banks look hundreds of yards away from where they used to be.

"Where are we going?" Simon asks nervously. All he sees is water.

"Just stay close and everything should be fine. Don't get off the path or you will be lost," Jenks replies. Simon follows closely behind as he is told. He looks down at the magical path below him. It's as if the horses were walking on water. He doesn't quite understand it.

They cross the lake safely and come to an immensely tall island that looks like it was placed there by the unknown. It is quite out of place, but they proceed along it until they reach a small cave opening. They go in. Simon is shocked to see a whole community residing inside.

"Now, you don't know anything about this, right Simon?" Jenks says and gives Simon a hard look.

"I only know we have a card game to play," Simon smirks.

They pass up a small corral of horses and Simon must hide his expression when he sees his stolen horse in the herd. They walk over to a dark corner where the locals from LaCrosse are playing cards.

"Welcome. We are glad to see you. Are you ready for us to take all your money again there, son?" one of the men asks Simon.

"Oh, we will see. We will see," Simon replies.

They drink and play cards for hours on end. As night falls, the island is completely pitch dark. It's darker than any time any of them can remember. As a dense fog rolls in over them, the locals get increasingly tense, so they call the game.

"We need to end this now. This feels like one of those nights we don't much like around here," Jenks says. Simon thinks this is very strange, but maybe it can be to his advantage.

"We get real spooked around here when the quiet and the darkness come. When the fog sets in, we stay tight and keep low," says Jenks.

As the locals seemingly slink away into the night, Simon sneaks out to the edge of the island. He can hear the sounds of the horses and senses this is the moment. He quietly mounts his horse and rides over to the corral. Luckily, no one is there. His horse walks right up to him. Simon tries the gate and it slips open easily. He grabs some rope and puts it gently around his stolen horse and leads both horses to what he thinks is the north end of the island.

He looks up at the night sky. Through an opening in the fog, he sees Polaris, the North Star. It is a comforting site. He knows he can proceed in that direction without encountering anyone else tonight. With much effort, Simon and the two horses fight their way back across the water to the north end of the lake. As the day breaks, they find a wooded grove, and they stop to rest.

After a few days, Simon and his horses make it back to Lomax Station. As they walk down the familiar lane, Simon sees Joshua standing at the door of the telegraph house.

“Well aren’t you a sight for sore eyes? We all thought you were long gone! How in the world did you find that horse?” Joshua asks.

“Well, let’s just say I was playing cards with amateurs,” and Simon gives a wily smile.

Joshua informs Simon of the good news. "You should know that the lab up north got back to us. The formula worked for them just like it did here. They instructed us to pump as much oil as we can. The experiment worked! Simon, I can't thank you enough," he says and extends his hand to Simon.

The men of the pumping station continue to work tirelessly under Joshua's command. Simon decides to stay around for a bit to learn as much as he can. He spends many weeks courting Adelaide. The next summer, they get married, move into town, and Simon continued his career.

"Wow, Grandma, horse thieves? That is unbelievable. Who would have thought the river could be so storied filled?"

"Yes, dear, that is the story I have been told for years. Oh, I see your mom is here now, you better get going. I will see you next weekend. We can have more fun with this geo thing."

"And you can tell me more stories!" Elisabeth hears her mom honking the car horn, so she says goodbye, hugs Ida, and hurries to the car.

Ida watches out the window until they pull away. She logs off the computer and heads up to the attic in her house. She rummages through some old things until she gets to an old trunk.

“There it is. I am glad I can still remember the important things,” she says to herself. It’s the old leather pouch. She opens it up to check inside. “I see it’s still in there,” she says. She draws the pouch tight and takes it downstairs to the parlor.

Chapter 6 The King

Another week goes by and it's Saturday once again. Ida has been waiting all morning to have Elisabeth over. Trinity pulls up and Elisabeth runs up the front porch steps and opens the door.

"Grandma! I'm here!"

"In here, dear."

Elisabeth rushes into the sitting room and sees Ida at the computer.

"Look, I have it all ready for you. I logged in and set up some neat finds. See, I even found the map page and got it to show me where we are. These are the ones I picked out. Aren't you proud of your grandma?" Ida says.

"Oh, yeah, cool, Grandma. You're really getting the hang of things. We need to print the map and I can also open it in my phone so we know where to go," Elisabeth says. They set off for the day. Ida drives to the caches while Elisabeth checks the map. Ida notices how quickly Elisabeth seems to find them now.

They are satisfied with the day's finds and head back home. It's just past lunch and Elisabeth says they need to stop and get something to eat. Elisabeth wants to go through a drive-thru.

"Well, ok dear, just for you. I really don't like those dastardly drive-thrus. They never get it right," Ida says.

They get their food and go back to Ida's house. Elisabeth logs their cache finds while Ida relaxes on the couch.

"I'm so glad you are good with that computer," Ida says.

"I like being on the computer. When I'm done, can you tell me more stories? Your stories are the best."

"Oh, well how about the time a prince came to the river to hunt for ducks?" Ida says and begins the story of the prince.

Everyone was truly thrilled when word came around that the Prince of Wales was coming from England to visit the river lands just to hunt. He arrived at the county line and made his way to the west by boat. He was surrounded by a large group of guards because people everywhere were trying to meet him. I think we know him as Prince Edward VII. He was quite the hunter. The people would come from far distances in hopes of seeing him, but he stayed far out of reach. He would float down the river and stop at campsites for a day or two. All the hunters who met him were thrilled. He stayed for weeks and everyone had a great time. At each place he stopped, he would tell a story of the King of England, George III, and the lore of a long, lost treasure, and it's rumored pilgrimage to the new land.

It was a long time ago. The supreme priest to the King of England was called to the castle. It was not a normal meeting with the king, so they went to a secluded room to discuss matters. King George III was very perplexed. He did not know how to parse the subject with the supreme priest, Thomas.

"Now, Thomas, I have a something weighing upon me in which I need to discuss with you. It must not ever leave this room. This information will surely return England to the great providence it is destined to be."

"Your Highness, I am true to the task and will remain vigilant to help you ascend to the height of governance. I will make sure everyone knows England is the superior nation."

"Well, Thomas," the King says, "I understand there is a treasure of great influence that is linked to the greatest man to ever walk upon this earth. I have it on great accord that this treasure is right here on this island of England. One citizen has possession of it and its influence is beyond their comprehension. Its exact position has slipped through any viceroy I have enacted to possess it. It must be brought in and its influence stabilized. In the wrong possession, it will be a threat to our very society and the prominence we know today. The last viceroy I dispatched left a cryptic note and has never been heard from since. You can read the note, but it cannot leave this palace. As King George hands Thomas the note, Thomas can see it is quite fragile, so he handles it with quiet care.

The note reads:

'The last I have known of the possible existence of the treasure, was that it was in the hands of a student priest in training. He crossed over from the mainland to study. The treasure was in a leather case. This case also held a length of rope. The leather did not appear to have been affected by age or the time it has transcended. The length of rope is of an unknown origin, but appears to have always been carried with the treasure, and it too has not been affected by age.'

"What do you think it could mean? Is there anything else that tells us where it might be?" the King asks.

"It is in the hands of the church and it seems the person holding the case is not truly aware of influence it has," Thomas says.

"I need you to go forth and find out who this student priest is. Investigate anyone who would have crossed over to England to finish their studies. Then we will dispatch our best guards to find the treasure. We must not fail! We must not falter! The entire respect of England rests upon us completing this task. My legacy as King and the economic transcendence of England depends on us completing this quest!" King George says.

"I will not falter nor tire until your command is complete, Your Highness. It is my honor to have bestowed upon me this quest."

Thomas leaves and the King returns to the throne room to finish his meeting with the knights of his court. Thomas embarks on a trip to the monastery to meet with the elders of the church, who take him to the records hall. Thomas is shown the latest roll call book to see where the last priests came from and where they were imparted to after they completed their training. It takes several days to scour the log books, but Thomas creates a final list of young priests who were signed in from either Spain or France.

There is one man of great intrigue that was from France. He was descended from a long history of church affiliation, but was a little older than the others when he entered into his training. His previous education was from a very exclusive university. Though he was highly intelligent, he didn't begin his training until he was done stabilizing his family's lands.

Ezekiel was his name. His distinguished career helped him finish in the monastery a year in advance of his entry class. He was then dispatched to a small town north of London, but his time was short there, and he was called out to the countryside to be an evangelist to the small villages. He is instructed to report back at times he deems necessary.

"Excuse me, Superior, has this Ezekiel reported back lately? Here is a log of his last location," Thomas asks.

"Let me see those log rolls. I see in these entries he has not been reported back since his departure. Your only other option is to check all the other logs to see if other evangelical brothers have reported seeing him. This room here houses the group of books that would hold all the latest reports. You are welcome to look them over for as long as you like," the Superior says.

"Thank you. I am truly thankful for your help and so is the King," Thomas says.

"I believe it was at that same time, Elisabeth, that one of your ancestors was out tending the family lands nearby," Ida says.

"Was it the priest that Thomas was looking for?"

"No. Not this particular man. This man's name was Enoch. He was larger than life. He was very, very tall and his shoulders were as wide as the day is long. Enoch was known throughout the local villages and was regarded as the best seaman that anyone had ever known. He had taken many voyages for many important businessmen. They say he once saved a ship in the midst of a terrible storm, and led the vessel and all aboard to safety. His voyages were legendary and many gathered far and wide to hear of his bravery."

Chapter 7 Enoch

It was a warm, sunny day when Enoch was out tending to the land. Over the distance, at the top of the hill, he saw his brother.

"Ezekiel! Ezekiel!" Enoch shouts. It was the loudest call anyone has ever heard. Ezekiel waves his arms, and rushes over to meet Enoch. As they embrace, Enoch lifts Ezekiel up over his head in joy.

"Whoa there, Brother! I need to live a little longer!" says Ezekiel.

"Hey, hey," Enoch says, "you are still small enough to throw around like a sack of potatoes." They smile and walk over to the main house. "What brings you back around here? It sure is great to see you," Enoch says. "Come, let's sit and have a drink. It's been a long day. It sure is great to have you back."

"It feels great to be home," says Ezekiel.

"What brings you back to the continent, Ezekiel?"

"I have been on sabbatical and crossing all over the lands as an emissary to the church in England. I'm sure you heard I was ordained in the church. After I was ordained, I had a calling to one church in particular. It went so well that the senior priest asked if I would go and evangelize on the mainland. It was a chance to get out and see the country, so I packed up and went to spread the word in every town and village. I went from town to town and before I knew it, I was near home. So, I figured it was a good place to stop and rest for the return trip back toward London. How has our family land been these days?" Ezekiel asks.

"It's been better since I got back and learned the flow of things. It's all worked out. I'm so proud of how you kept the place going when I left. You made it easy for me to return. The place runs without a hitch, so there's not much for me to do other than keep things in order," Enoch says.

"I did what I had to do. I knew you had no choice but to go on that voyage to Spain and make the trips for the tradesmen. I knew we had to let you go make the money. You were the best man for the voyage," Ezekiel says.

"Yes, it was an opportunity I had to do. It paid well. I believe now that I was supposed to be there through the tough times when no one else would have overcome that dire trip. There were several times when things were at their lowest. I knew the chance for the whole ship to go down was almost assured."

"That's when they needed you the most, Enoch."

"Brother, I feared for all our lives, but I knew I had to be strong and have the faith of the Lord because we had more left to do on this earth. We barely made it through. I heard some boats just in front of us never made it back to port." Enoch sighs and hangs his head. "I clearly remember the day we pulled into the trading port. Every single man standing on the dock welcomed us like we were royalty. They had heard how bad the storms were, and many ships were late and feared never to be heard from again. But, we sailed in just like it was a calm lake we had just conquered."

"You sure brought us the help we needed back here, Enoch. The money we received helped us overcome the toughest of times. When problems seemed insurmountable, it was your finances we used to stay alive. The other families were not doing so well. We would have not either if it wasn't for your sacrifice out there. That is the only way I would have been able to work our family's land to the point it is now," Ezekiel says.

Ezekiel takes a look around the lush, green countryside. "Where is our brother, Joseph? I haven't seen him in a blue moon."

"Ah, Joseph, well, he has gotten to be quite the helping hand and has grown up strong. Not as strong as I, but he is a good, smart worker." Enoch laughs. "He has worked hard to learn everything around here. Sometimes, I think he only needs me around for his own amusement. I think he could run the place all by himself."

"That's so good to hear, Brother, I was surely hoping you weren't doing everything by yourself," says Ezekiel.

They talk through the night. In the morning, Ezekiel tells Enoch that he must go. He has a calling to finish, but he assures Enoch he will make it back soon.

Many days pass. One day, Enoch and Joseph are tending the flock in the field when they see three riders on the horizon. There are two larger riders covered in heavy armor, flanking a smaller one, who is dressed in a royal uniform. Their armor is blinding in the sun. The trio approaches Enoch and Joseph and asks to speak with them. Enoch invites them to the main house.

"What can we do for you?" Enoch asks.

"We have been dispatched from the King. We are seeking the priest, Ezekiel. We have been all over the countryside and our information has brought us here," the man in the royal uniform says.

"Is there some sort of trouble?" Joseph asks cautiously.

"We have been dispatched by the King to inform Ezekiel that he is needed at once. He is to report immediately to the English cathedral for a very important gathering of the highest officials of the royal cabinet."

Enoch has a worried look and the man continues. "It is of the utmost importance that we locate the priest, Ezekiel. We will not report back without learning his whereabouts. Have you been hearing from him?"

The man is very serious and Enoch is nervous. "He is not here now, but he was here a while ago. He left early one morning. He said he had to follow the Lord's path and continue his mission," Enoch says. "He didn't say where he was going."

With a stern face, the man says, "If he does come back, be very quiet about the importance of our meeting. Send him back to the trading port on the east coast. Tell him to send a dispatch to alert us when he has arrived there. We will accompany him to the palace. He must wait until we meet him."

"Yes, we can do that, please travel safely," Enoch says and shows the men to the door.

The riders make a brisk exit, and journey off towards the west.

"What was that about, Enoch?"

"I don't know, but I get the feeling it was not all good." Enoch thinks to himself for a minute then says to Joseph, "I think you need to wait a couple of days. Then take our best horse and ride to the towns southwest of here. Ezekiel would surely have gone there and the villagers might know where he was headed. Maybe he ended up at the church that lies to the south. Be very careful not to let on who you are. Just say that you had heard him speak and were so inspired that you decided to travel with him. If you see those riders again, make your way to a different town, as if you are going to do some trading."

"I will go and try to catch up to Ezekiel and bring him back here," Joseph says.

"Joseph, please be careful," replies Enoch.

Enoch helps Joseph prepare his horse and he heads off to the southwest as Enoch instructed. He rides fast and is soon out of sight over the rolling meadow.

Chapter 8 Ezekiel

It takes three days for Joseph to get to the three villages west of home. At each village he stops at, the people all know of Ezekiel and his message of Christ. Each time, they help Joseph stay on track with his quest to find his brother.

He comes to a town where there is a large, old church. Joseph rides up to the massive, wooden door. It's not locked, so he enters quietly into the sanctuary. He sees a woman tending to the altar, and asks if she knows Ezekiel. She is very weary and eyes him cautiously to make sure he is who he says he is. Convinced of his identity, she escorts him up a rear stairwell to a small sanctuary room.

As the woman opens the door, Joseph sees him sitting at a desk, writing, and working diligently. "Ezekiel!" Joseph says.

Ezekiel turns around and jumps up immediately. "Oh, it's so good to see you! I prayed that you would come looking for me. I have word there are royal guards dispatched on a mission to get me back to London under King George's orders. I have been in England long enough to know that is not normal. I don't think it's in my best interest to go back. I couldn't return home either, because I know you are being watched."

"Yes, that is what Enoch and I feared, so I waited for a while until I came looking for you," Joseph says. "I made sure I wasn't followed and I doubled back several times to see if anyone was tracking me."

"Well done, Brother. We need to go now and make haste toward home," Ezekiel says.

"Are you sure? They will be watching for you to return."

"I am sure, Joseph. We need to go home to secure the future. We will be stealthy in our journey. Trust in God, and me," says Ezekiel.

They mount their horses loaded up with provisions, and make their way home to Enoch. It takes several days since they circle back many times to make sure they are not being followed.

It is a calm, brisk day as they break the crest of the rolling meadow and see the main house. The chimney is billowing smoke and all is quiet. They hurriedly put their horses into the stable and slip in through the back door of the house. As soon as they open the door, Enoch instantly appears in defense, not knowing his brothers have returned.

"Hold it there, Brother! It's only us," Ezekiel says.

Enoch drops his weapon in great relief and embraces them. “I’ve been ready for those riders to come back. It’s been tough on me to be alone waiting for you two.”

They seat themselves in the main gathering room of the house, in front of the blazing fireplace. Enoch folds his hands across his chest and looks at Joseph and Ezekiel.

“We need to decide what to do,” Enoch says.

“I think there is only one choice, Enoch. You and your family need to pack up and leave here under the pretense of going to the new land. You should get on the next charter that departs from the coast. I am sure you can make the case that you are making the journey on business. Tell them it’s a long way across the Atlantic, so you brought your family along for company,” Ezekiel says. “When you get to the new land, you will need to move west until you are safe to start a new life. Joseph, you need to stay here to run our family’s land as it should be run. You know what to do.”

“I need to know why they are looking for you, Ezekiel,” Joseph says.

Finally, Ezekiel tells them why he is being sought after. “It’s best you now know why. They are looking for a treasure that they believe our family has, but we do not have it. They truly believe we possess it and will not stop until they get it. You see, our oldest ancestor that we know of is Simon Stone.” Ezekiel looks at Joseph intently. “Simon Stone, the Apostle.”

“The same Simon that was an Apostle of Jesus? Are you sure of this?” Joseph asks in disbelief.

“Yes, the very same one. That is why they will never believe we do not have the treasure,” says Ezekiel.

“Then God will give me the strength to keep the family land secure while you are away. I am up to the task. I will remain steadfast in my mission,” Joseph says.

They all go off to get some sleep and wait for morning.

Enoch and Ezekiel wake early before the sun rises. They go to the cellar of the storage building. They quietly move the pantry shelves to reveal a hole carved out of the stone wall.

“Here it is,” Ezekiel says. He hands it to Enoch. “You must keep this secure on your person at all times. You must keep it secret and unknown to anyone in the new world. It is up to you to keep it safe.”

“Yes, I will keep it safe,” Enoch says. Enoch carefully removes the leather pouch from inside the chest and places it securely in his coat. They replace the pantry shelves and go pack the wagon for the trip to the coast.

Enoch and his family arrive at the trading port. Enoch’s reputation is widely known and he soon secures a position as an assistant to the captain of a ship bound for America. They board the ship with all of their worldly goods to begin the three month voyage.

It is a journey typical of the long crossing, with multiple storms and close, cramped quarters. Enoch does well for the captain and his crew and they arrive safely with all souls well. Enoch and his family leave the port and travel west to a small farming town. They stay at a local lodge until Enoch procures a tract of land suitable for farming. It does not take him long to get the farm up to production. He builds the small homestead even larger to provide enough room for his family and farm hands.

Ezekiel leaves Joseph and goes to meet with the royal guards and on to the supreme priest and the King. Ezekiel knows his fate, but he must protect his family and the treasure. He must ensure Enoch's safe passage to the new world.

The guards treat him well and soon they arrive in London to meet with the hierarchy. Ezekiel is questioned concertedly because not one of the interrogators believes he has no knowledge of the treasure. Ezekiel is led to a small cell and placed under lock and key. The guards watch him closely. Ezekiel spends many nights praying for his brothers, because he knows the King has issued the order of inquisition. The King will not rest until he has the treasure in his possession.

Chapter 9 Joseph

Nearly a year later, Joseph goes into town to purchase some farming tools and seeds for the spring planting. He is strolling down the wooden walkway in front of the store, when a stranger begins walking closely next to him. He senses something is wrong, but keeps going to see the outcome of this encounter. The stranger keeps pace with Joseph, all the while looking forward.

"Joseph Stone?" the stranger says. Joseph nods. The stranger continues, "I have a message of utmost importance. You have a brother, a priest, who is being held in silence at the church in London. He is well, but has been held captive for months. I have been given instructions to tell you he needs your help to get him to a safe place now, and for the rest of his days. It is of grave importance that Ezekiel is relieved from his prison, as the patience of the King is nigh." Just as quickly as the stranger appeared, he was gone.

Joseph rides back to the farmland and calls on his head steward to discuss some things of importance.

"I have called on you to tell you I have a mission of grave importance that I must complete. I am leaving and will not be back," Joseph says.

“Ever?” the steward asks.

“No, never. I will never return. I entrust the land to you. Keep it in good order. I have drawn up the deed that gives you sole ownership and we will never be back to contest it. If anyone should come and ask about me or my family, tell them I was the last one left and that I went off to explore the eastern continents. I have enough money to make it a long time, so I won’t ask anything from you. My family and I are giving you full ownership of the land in thanks for your years of service to us. We trust you will take care of it in a prudent fashion,” Joseph says.

Joseph seals the deed scroll and hands it to the steward.

“Well, sir, I thank you for everything and I will do my best to honor your family in all I do with the lands. I bid you safe passage and I hope to find you well someday,” the steward says.

“And I to you,” Joseph says.

Joseph packs all the important family goods on the wagon and sets out on his journey east to the trading port.

As soon as Joseph arrives at the port, he dispatches a letter to Enoch, who is in the new world, asking that he return as soon as possible, as there is a matter of grave importance. It costs him triple to make sure the letter is stayed in the right hands and makes it to Enoch without any royal notice.

It takes eight more months of waiting, but Joseph is finally there at the port to greet the next ship from America. He can see Enoch standing tall on the bow as it floats into port. Enoch is still larger than life. It seems as though he can single handedly pull the ship to dock with the tow rope.

The entire crew thanks Enoch as he departs. Enoch and Joseph walk across the docks and mount a couple of horses to ride to the house Joseph has rented. As they ride, Enoch expresses his concern to Joseph.

"I gathered from your letter that it was truly important that I made my way back as soon as I could," Enoch says.

"Yes, Brother, as you can see, Ezekiel is not with me. I wrote you because I need your help," Joseph pleads.

"Ezekiel? Is he in trouble?" Enoch says with a worried, rough tone.

"Yes, I have it on great accord he is being held captive of sorts at the Church of England's cathedral in London. Soon those responsible will not be so willing to wait. You see, the King of England's reigning years are waning and the economic times are bad. The King is purported of needing a way of leaving a legacy of solid reign to his heir. Since I've been here, I have found out that the King believes there is a treasure from biblical times that can help him turn England around. I think the King believes Ezekiel knows where it is," Joseph says.

"Oh, Joseph, you have grown so wise these past years. I am glad you summoned me back to England. Ezekiel will never let the King know the whereabouts of the treasure. You must know I can assure you it is safe in the new world. I knew it had to be taken as far away as possible to ensure its safety."

"What do you think we should do? I am willing to do whatever you want, no matter the outcome," Joseph says.

"We are going to go get Ezekiel, and take him to a place of safety for all time," Enoch says.

Enoch and Joseph hire a trader to ship their worldly goods to a small town off the coast of

France, where he will store the goods for safe keeping until they return. The brothers make their way for London and take care not to be noticed in their travels. As soon as they arrive in the south suburbs of London, they worship in a couple of churches. While in the churches, they collect information on the whereabouts of Ezekiel. They find out he is living in a small part of a campus belonging to the Church of England in London and it is not guarded in force.

They learn Ezekiel is allowed to walk the grounds freely, but no further. After watching for a few days, they learn the timing of the happenings on the campus. They find some robes to disguise themselves, and formulate a plan.

It is late one afternoon, just at dusk. They walk to the garden and see Ezekiel meditating as he walks. They wait until the moment they will not be seen by anyone in the parish and make their move. Ezekiel breaks from his calm and knows immediately who they are. He follows them quietly to the horses they have hitched nearby.

The three brothers ride swiftly through the night and make their way to the westernmost dock. Their passage is already secured and they voyage to the French Coast. When they arrive, they procure new horses and ride to the place they have stored their belongings. In a few weeks, they get to a small town in northern France, where Enoch purchases a suitable home with a vineyard for himself and his brothers.

It takes a few months, but Enoch, Ezekiel, and Joseph are successful at keeping the vineyard running well. Joseph still has concerns the King will not let any time or distance get in the way of finding them and the day will come when they will be too obvious to miss. He begins to think he should return to England to establish some contact with the local villages so that he can be aware of the quest to find Ezekiel. He knows of a town called Spondon. It would be a good place to stay that would still be far enough away to not draw attention. Enoch and Ezekiel agree to his plan, so Joseph travels back to Spondon, England, to stay aware of the search for Ezekiel.

A car horn honks, jerking Ida out of her story, and back to the present. She looks outside to see Trinity waiting in the car, waving to her.

"Well, dear, we have to stop there because I see your mom is outside and she looks like she is in a hurry," Ida says.

"Can't we tell her to come back later? It was just getting good," Elisabeth says.

“Yes, I know it was, but I am a little worn out and need a break. I should get some rest. I’m not as young as you think I am,” Ida says.

“Oh, ok, but will you tell me more later? You promise?”

“Of course, dear, we will definitely continue this another time,” Ida says.

Elisabeth packs up her things and says goodbye. Ida watches them pull away. Telling Elisabeth all these memories sure brings the stories back to life. She smiles to herself while she lies down to rest, and dreams of all she has known. It’s a restful sleep we all enjoy once in a great while.

Chapter 10 Spondon

A few days pass and the phone rings at Ida's house. "Hello," she answers. "Oh, it's you, dear, how are things? I was hoping to hear from you to see if maybe Elisabeth, my dear granddaughter, could come over. I enjoy her company so much," Ida says.

"Well, Mom, that's what I'm calling about. Elisabeth keeps going on and on about this story of our relatives from a long time ago. She has so many grand tales and plots that I almost can't believe her, but she has never once been untruthful before, so that's why I am calling," Trinity says.

"You know I have been getting long in the tooth, and I need to tell her these stories before I forget them. She seems to enjoy them. They have been passed down for generations, and have never changed, so who am I to say they are not true," Ida says.

"What about the one about Prince Edward VII and King George III?" Trinity says.

"Oh, yes, those are good ones. I was told that story partly came from your great, great, Grandpa Simon, and partly from the known stories of when the Prince of Wales came to our area to hunt a long time ago," Ida says.

"What? You mean a prince came to hunt in our area? That must have been some hunting," Trinity says.

"Yes, I am sure of that, because it was reported in the news that he was here. It was a great to do back then."

"Elisabeth sure likes hearing you tell the stories, Mom. Can I come over next time? I would like to know more myself. We should make a day of it," Trinity says.

"Of course, that would be swell. I look forward to seeing you both," Ida says.

It's a sunny, beautiful Saturday. Ida woke up early and is waiting patiently for Elisabeth and Trinity to arrive. She has made some crumpets and set out her best tea. She has waited all week and cannot remember a time she has been so impatient for them to get there.

Ida is watching out the window and finally sees them. Elisabeth nearly jumps out of the car before it is completely stopped, runs toward the house, and bursts through the door.

"I'm ready to hear more stories!" Elisabeth says.

"Whoa, hold on, dear. Wait for your mom to come in. She wants to listen, too. You have her more excited about the stories then I thought possible," Ida says.

Trinity comes in and sees that Ida has already put out tea and crumpets on the coffee table. Ida pours herself a cup of hot tea, sits back in her easy chair, and wraps her favorite afghan around herself.

Trinity is ready to burst with anticipation. "Don't leave us hanging! What happened after Joseph moved to Spondon?" Trinity asks. So, Elisabeth did repeat it correctly to her mother, Ida thinks.

Ida gets comfortable and gathers her thoughts. "Let me see, Joseph moved into a small house in Spondon, England," begins Ida, and she tells Trinity and Elisabeth the story.

Joseph had set himself up with a small machine shop in Spondon. He was a very talented mechanic, so he fixed all sorts of contraptions to make money. Spondon was a small town near the west coast of England. The town was a suitable size to allow Joseph to make a living and blend in as a new citizen. He fit in well, and the townspeople quickly grew fond of him because he could help anyone with his knowledge of all things mechanical.

It was not long before Joseph was supplying the local merchants with his equipment. One day, he was delivering a potato peeler to the local butcher shop. This peeler was able to skin large quantities of potatoes at one time and the shop used it to make all sorts of salads and dishes. It was a very large machine and tough to carry. To say it was cumbersome was being nice. He struggled dearly to carry it off the wagon and into the butcher shop.

"Hello, Joe! Good to see you. Let me give you a hand with that. Boy, are we in desperate need of that peeler. Our orders are backed up for days. People are going to start revolting on me like it was the French Revolution!" the butcher says.

"I get the joke there, limey fellow!" Joseph says. He and the butcher share a loud, hearty laugh.

"Father? Is everything ok? I heard a loud ruckus."

An exceptionally stunning young woman comes through the curtain from the back of the store. Joseph looks up at her and is left standing in awe.

"Joe, this is my daughter, Amelia," says the butcher.

"Uh, hello, good to meet you," Joseph says.

The butcher hands Joseph his payment. "Well, Joe, this should be enough to cover the cost of the peeler. It's working great."

"Thank you," says Joseph. "If you need anything else, you know where to find me."

"Sure do," the butcher says and shakes Joseph's hand.

"Nice to meet you, Joseph, don't be a stranger now," Amelia says.

The days pass by. Joseph works in his machine shop and with the butcher at the local festivals. Joseph and Amelia become close, and Joseph asks permission to court Amelia. Soon they marry, and have a son and daughter. Joseph's business grows and their life together is as simple and normal as most lives can be.

“Mom, what about Enoch and Ezekiel? What happens to Enoch’s family in America?” Trinity asks.

“Oh, dear, I’m getting to that part,” Ida says.

In a matter of months, the vineyard is running smoothly. Enoch and Ezekiel work hard to build a place for Ezekiel to live out his days in peace. They build a house and set up the vineyard with enough grape vines and livestock to maintain a sustainable harvest for years.

When Enoch feels that Ezekiel will be safe and able to live without fear, he tells him he must leave the vineyard. Ezekiel is saddened, and he thanks Enoch for all he has done for him. He knows that Enoch must make his way to the East trading coast and find a charter going to America, so that he can be with his family.

Enoch is too large a man not to be noticed in France. America is the safest place for him to stay out of reach of the monarchy. There, in America, is where he will guard the treasure. Ezekiel bids Enoch goodbye. In his heart he knows it’s the last time he will see his brother, until they meet again in infinity.

Enoch makes a safe journey across the Atlantic and finds his family well. They live out their days running their farm. They prosper and help others who have made the trip to the new world. Occasionally, English guards pass by and try to question Enoch's family, but their influence is meaningless here, and Enoch has supporters of all facets in his defense. The guards dare not intimidate Enoch or his family for fear of their own lives.

"Grandma, don't forget about the prince! What happened to the prince? Did he really come to the Kankakee to hunt?" Elisabeth asks.

"He came here under the pretense to hunt, but he had other plans in mind," Ida says. "He was really looking for your ancestors and the treasure. He was taking a chance coming here, but this was the last place he could trace them to. Oh, he tried hard to find our heirs. He ran down the rivers, and carried a group of admirers along the way. He must have realized his information was not as good as he thought, because he left quickly one day."

The prince was at a hunting camp when a courier came to him. He was handed a note from a royal guard that ordered him to return to England at once, because the President of the United States had instructed his security force to act immediately to find the prince. The security forces are to escort the prince to the Capitol to discuss his true reason for being in America and more specifically the Kankakee River hunting grounds. The President is demanding to know the truth behind the prince's diplomacy. The President seems to think the prince is out to find some sort of great treasure in America, and abscond back to England with it. If this is the case, the prince will be retained, and not allowed to leave American shores. The President will not allow any sort of takeover by England while he is in office.

So, Prince Edward made haste and quietly escaped America in short order.

"Oh, Mom, that is the most amazing story you've ever told me. I hope my memory is half as good as yours when I'm your age," Trinity says.

"Trinity, it has to be. That is our past, and it's too important to forget," Ida says.

Trinity and Elisabeth get ready to go home. Trinity tells Ida she will pick her up on Tuesday to take her to her doctor appointment.

"I will be ready. Not willing, but ready," Ida says. "Have a great week at school, Elisabeth."

Ida gives Elisabeth a hug, and kisses her goodbye.

Chapter 11 George

It's Tuesday and Trinity takes Ida to the doctor. Ida has never liked doctors. She has been healthy her whole life and never worried about anything until lately. For the first time in her life, she's been struggling to get a good night's rest. Her mind is sound, but her body has not been like it was.

Trinity sits in the waiting room while Ida goes back to meet the doctor. After about twenty minutes, Ida comes out and Trinity asks her how it went.

"It went just fine, dear, nothing new. Just like last time," Ida says.

"Oh, that's good. Don't forget to make your next appointment with the nurse before we leave," Trinity says.

"No, it's not necessary. The doctor isn't requesting one."

"Well, ok, it went better than I thought. I'm glad everything went well," Trinity says.

"Yes, dear, I will be fine," says Ida.

Trinity helps Ida to the car and they drive back to Ida's house. Ida makes her way to the parlor and sits down to relax for a spell.

Ida is very comfortable in her reclining chair. She thinks back to the days she had with her dad, George. He was a tall man, with a very solid demeanor. He was known for his integrity and candor.

There was one day in particular that she remembers vividly. It was an early morning and her dad was out scraping the frost off the car while he waited for the engine to warm up. It was late winter, almost spring, and the sunshine was trying to bring a little warmth to the air. Ida was watching her dad from the parlor window. All of a sudden, the car stops running. George stops scraping and immediately jumps into the driver's seat. He tries to restart it, again and again, without success. He finally gets out, slams the car door, and stomps up the porch.

He walks in the door and Ida's mom asks what's wrong. He tells her that the car just up and quit. No warning, just up and quit. He is so frustrated, but he keeps his composure, and grabs the phone.

“Hello, Irma? Could you get me the number for Tom’s Auto? Thank you,” George speaks calmly.

His friend, Tom, comes over to check the car. It doesn’t look good to Ida, who is watching them from inside. Then a tow truck arrives. Tom hooks up the car and tows it away. George comes back in the house, looking beat down, and speaks with Ida’s mom in a tone too quiet for Ida to hear.

Ida’s mom walks down to the corner store to pick up some groceries for dinner. George is sitting in the parlor, listening to the radio. Ida creeps in and asks if there’s anything wrong.

“Now, we have to get the car fixed. It will cost a lot of money, and times are so tight right now,” George says. “But, don’t worry, Little Ida, your dad will find a way to get it fixed. Don’t you worry,” George says.

Ida goes to her room to find a book to read. Her door is open just enough for her to see her parent’s room. She looks and sees her dad, standing at his bureau, holding a leather pouch. He is crying.

Ida goes across the hall to him. He turns as he hears her come in the room, and tries to wipe his tears so his daughter won’t see.

"What's wrong, Dad?"

"Oh, my Little Ida, everything is better. It's a miracle. Everything will be fine now, and most likely forever."

"How, Dad?"

"Well, I think you are old enough, and I know you are wise enough, so I will tell you now," George says. He holds his hands out to Ida. "This is a leather pouch. It's a very, very, old, leather pouch."

"It doesn't look that old," Ida says.

"You must understand it is older than either of us can imagine. It belonged to one of our oldest relatives, Simon Stone. It is hundreds of years old.

"I've only heard that name Simon in church. He's in the Bible. It can't be the same man," Ida says.

"Yes, I was told it is the same man from the Bible, Simon Peter, the Apostle," George says.

"Can we see what's inside?" Ida asks.

Inside the pouch is a length of string and a Roman coin.

"I've never seen a coin like that, Dad, but the man on it looks like Caesar," Ida says.

"Yes, he does look like Caesar, Caesar of Rome. I've been told this is not just any Roman coin, but it is the most sought after Roman coin in the world," George says.

"I do remember a little from Sunday school, a bible verse talking about giving something to Caesar?" Ida asks.

"Yes, it goes, 'Render unto Caesar the things which are Caesar's, and unto God the things that are God's'," George says.

"But, Jesus touched the coin when he said that," Ida says. "It can't be the same one."

"Yes, I've been told this is the same coin, the very same coin that was in the hands of Jesus Christ himself. I have always wondered if it was true, but now I believe it," George says.

"You see, we had no way to pay for the car to be fixed, so I came up here to go through our finances to find any possible way to pay for it. I was looking through the drawer when I ran across the leather pouch. I lifted up the pouch, and underneath it was more than enough money to fix the car!" George says.

"Now, Ida, this has been in our family a very long time. I received it the day after your grandpa passed away. I was at his house, sorting through his effects, and I found an old trunk. It looked old enough to have come over from France with the Stone family. There were some really old items in it. Then I saw this leather pouch near the bottom. It was wrapped in a lush, velvet fabric. It stood out like a gold nugget in a stream!" George says.

"I opened the fabric to find this leather pouch. The leather was not like anything I had ever seen. When I looked inside it, I found this length of string and the coin. It looked like something truly important, so I kept it around," says George.

"Later, I remembered some stories of a family treasure, that I was told when I was younger. I kept the pouch with me for weeks and carried it everywhere I went. Looking back, those were the best weeks of our lives. We had no shortage of money and everything we did together felt just magical. After a while, I got so busy, I put the pouch away in the bureau to keep it safe. I only came across it occasionally, and when I did, it seemed each time whatever problems we were having disappeared. I never thought twice about it," George says.

“I did some research on the leather. It is goat skin leather. Normally, goat skin is of a peasant quality. It doesn’t wear well, and has a short lifespan. That was the most curious thing, because this goat skin leather pouch doesn’t look like it was worn at all,” says George.

“I knew this was the coin from the Roman days of Caesar. My dad passed before he could finish the whole story, but I pieced it together from what he and my family were able to tell me. I never believed any of them, because the tales seemed too good to be true, but I believe now,” George says.

“Ida, you need to keep this to yourself from now until you know it’s time to tell someone. When that day comes, you will be certain, as I knew today was the day to tell you. Someday soon, I will pass this treasure to you to keep safe. I was not the staunchest believer in the coin until today. Yes, times were hard, but somehow we always made it through. It’s been this way all throughout my days, as far back as I can remember, our family has been alright,” says George.

“Yes, Dad, I have wondered the same things, at different times, but I would never have believed in anything other than karma,” Ida says.

“Me too, but the more I tried not to believe, the more I would be drawn to it. I wonder if I had trusted it sooner, would things have been a little better early on. Some of your great relatives had a stronger faith and their lives seemed so much simpler,” George says.

“Dad, I love you so much! I will cherish this moment forever. I will never forget.”

Ida never forgot that day with her dad. That day brought them closer together than they had ever been. They became inseparable until the day George passed on.

The phone rings waking Ida up. She is able to answer it in time. It’s Elisabeth calling to tell her she will be over again on Saturday. Ida is so happy to hear Elisabeth’s voice. They talk for a bit, say goodbye, and Ida shuffles back to her chair. What a good sleep, she thinks, and gently closes her eyes again.

Chapter 12 Attorney

Saturday arrives once again. The morning brings soft, warm dew settling on the grass. Ida watches out the window as she waits for Elisabeth. She looks around at the neighborhood and remembers all it used to be. It wasn't a wealthy area, but definitely a proud one. The lawns were perfectly manicured and the homes well kept. The garages were nicely painted and the roofs were never in disrepair. The sidewalks were edged. The driveways, though stone, never bore a weed, and neither did the deep, green lawns. Ida recalls the melody of children playing in the summer sun. It looks very different now.

The familiar crackle of car tires on gravel gets her attention. There is Trinity, pulling up, and letting Elisabeth out. Ida is moving quicker than normal today, and beats Elisabeth to the door. Elisabeth rushes in and gives Ida a huge hug.

"What a great hug you give your grandma, dear. Thank you so much. What on earth did I do to deserve that?" asks Ida.

"Oh nothing, Grandma, I'm just so happy to see you! I have been waiting too many days to get back here. I am under strict orders to tell Mom your stories when I get home, as best I can. She really wanted to come today, but she has appointments to go to," Elisabeth says.

"Well, we will be fine on our own today. I'm so sorry, but story time will have to wait a while. I have a special day set for us, but I need to stop at the attorney's office first, so stay suited up. Let me grab my purse and keys and we can go," Ida says.

"You can tell me stories while you drive."

"Ok, dear, I can do that," Ida says.

Ida drives to her attorney's office. They wait their turn, and then go in. It's a typical, old fashioned office, with walnut covered walls throughout, and they smell of the past.

"What can we do for you today, Ida? Please, sit down," the attorney says.

"I am here to revise my will, so it's up to date. I have drafted what I would like to do. Will you please have a look to make sure it makes sense? Here, I printed it out for you," Ida says.

"You did this by yourself? Is she your secret?" asks the attorney. He motions to Elisabeth sitting next to Ida.

“No, this is Elisabeth, my granddaughter. You haven’t seen her in a while,” Ida says.

“Oh, yes, she has grown very quickly. You’ve done a fine job helping your grandmother with this,” the attorney says. Ida and Elisabeth look at each other and chuckle.

“I didn’t help her. She did it by herself. My Grandma is amazing!” Elisabeth says.

“Thank you. I did type it myself and even got the printer thing to work right. I was so proud of myself,” Ida says.

“Well! I am truly amazed with you, Ida. You did this all on your own? I think I need to offer you a job,” says the attorney.

“Oh, please, I am too old to keep up with your office. Besides, it runs so smoothly, I would only mess it up,” Ida says.

The attorney takes a look at the document given to him by Ida. “Let’s see what you have here. I see you haven’t changed your will in about ten years. Has it been that long? It looks like you’ve been very specific and this should clearly define your intentions. So far, it looks good. I will have the secretary notarize your signature. I will make any changes if needed, and you can stop by to review them," the attorney says.

"That sounds very good. Thank you for all your help over the years. My family and I are truly indebted," Ida says.

"You're welcome, Ida. It is always an honor to help you. After all, you have done so much over the years for me, my family, and the community. You are truly a treasure to know," the attorney says.

They say goodbye and Ida and Elisabeth return to the car. As they pull out to the intersection, Elisabeth is ready to hear more tales. "Grandma, can you tell me more about the past? Tell me anything. Your stories are so surreal and they make me so happy."

Ida checks her rearview mirrors for traffic, and begins where she last left off.

Prince Edward high tailed it out of America before the President's security detail got to him, and returned safely to England. Soon after, the Queen dispatched him to the East. He was sent on a mission to look for clues to the whereabouts of the treasure. The royal guards were failing in their pursuit, and the prince was sent to replace them.

England was not in the best of times and things weren't looking good. His mother, the Queen, thought his ability to make friends in dire times could help him find new leads in the search. He continued to look for the mysterious treasure of good fortune. He traveled to the British Isles, then to Jerusalem, and all the countries in between.

He did make a lot of new acquaintances and even uncovered some information about the treasure's past, but its present trail eluded him, and he returned to England hopeless. The royal guards were kept on dispatch to scour the European continent in hopes of finding something. Time passed, and England braved through, but never returned to its former worldwide glory.

"I do remember some stories about Joseph and his family. They fared well in Spondon and became an integral part of the community. They never achieved a high status, but were comfortable being middle class, and Joseph made sure they were always well taken care of."

Ida drove a few miles before she turned at the home furnishing store. "We need to stop here, so I can get some things," Ida says.

"Sure, Grandma, that would be fine."

Chapter 13 Vessels

Ida drives slowly through the parking lot of the home furnishing store until she finds an empty spot close to the door. Once inside, they peruse the kitchen department and look at the dishes.

"There is so much to look at here. I remember when there were only a few different patterns to choose from. There are so many now, I can buy exactly what I want, and they're not too expensive, either. Let's look over here in this aisle, Elisabeth. I am looking for a strong, sealed container, about medium size," says Ida.

"For a geocache, Grandma?"

"Well, maybe. That would be a good idea," Ida says.

"How about this plastic one? It is about the size of a quart," Elisabeth says.

"That looks close to what I want, except it needs a strong, sealed lid."

"I forgot. Geocaches get wet, don't they? It can't be sunny all the time," Elisabeth says.

"How about that one," Ida says. "Can you get it, dear? Yes, the clear one, with the blue stripes." Elisabeth reaches up to the top shelf and hands the container down to Ida.

"It says it's water tight. That is what I'm looking for. How may do they have?" Ida asks.

"There are six on the shelf, but I see a box of them over there," Elisabeth says.

"Grab that box, please, dear. This should work well as a geo thingy!"

"Yes, Grandma. It's called a geocache, and it will be perfect."

"Let's take our loot up to the cashier, and check out," Ida says.

They pay for their stuff, load it into the trunk, and drive back home. Elisabeth carries the box of containers into the kitchen, and lines them up across the counter.

"Let's see, what do we need to put in there? A sign-in log for people to write their name, a pencil, and something to trade," Elisabeth says.

Ida looks around, and has an idea. She opens the hall closet, and looks at all the stuff crammed in the shelves. "How about a game piece from my

Parcheesi game?" she asks. "What's your favorite color?"

"Blue! Blue!" Elisabeth says. "Great idea, Grandma, that's my favorite game."

They put all the items in the container. Elisabeth prints out a flyer that tells the finder to go to www.geojamboree.com to log in the date of their find.

"Close it up tight, Elisabeth, it needs to be waterproof."

"I got it on good and tight for you," Elisabeth says.

Just as they are finishing, Trinity pulls up. "I have to go now, but next time we will go put that geocache out," Elisabeth says. "Don't do it without me!"

"I will wait for you, dear, it will be truly fun. I will see you next weekend, and maybe your mom can go along, too," Ida says.

Ida sits down at the computer, and it comes out of sleep mode. She logs into her www.geojamboree.com account. She finds the handouts and flyers section of the website, and prints out a geoletter. The geoletter will tell the finder about the cache, and where they can log it in. There is a place on the website to write about what they found, and what items they traded.

Then she opens the word processing program and types up some letters. Some letters will go into safe deposit boxes and others will go into the sealed containers. She does a search for Lloyd's of London to get some contact information. They have a telephone number, and an email. She decides to use the email contact. After she composes the message, she sends it to the printer. As the printer whirs away, she gets her things to go out.

Ida drives alone to her bank, and finds a parking spot near the front door. When she enters the bank, she sees a friendly face she has known for years.

"It's good to see you, Ida. How have you been?" her friend asks.

"I have been well, thank you. I need your help with the safe deposit boxes," Ida says.

"Right over here. Do you have your key?"

"Oh, no, I need to rent a couple of new ones," Ida says. "One needs to be about the size of a shoebox, and the other only needs to hold an envelope."

"We can do that. Just fill out this paperwork, and I will take you back to the vault," her friend says. Ida completes the forms, and gets the keys to the two new boxes. The vault attendant helps her unlock the large box, and takes Ida to the privacy booth.

"When you are done, just push this button to turn the ready light on," the attendant says.

The vault attendant leaves Ida alone in the booth. She opens her purse. Ida pulls out the leather pouch and puts it in the large box. Then she puts the letter in the small box. She closes them, and pushes the button for the light.

In no time, the attendant appears, and helps Ida place the boxes back in their slots in the vault.

"There you go, Ida. All locked up tight. Keep your keys safe and we will keep the permission cards here. Only the people named on the cards will be allowed access, and only then if they have the keys," her friend says.

"Yes, I will make sure of it. Thank you for your help. Have a wonderful day," Ida says. She leaves the bank, and walks around the corner to the copy shop.

The bell chimes when she opens the door of the shop. All at once, the familiar smell of the copy machines fills the air.

"May I help you?" the cashier asks.

"Hello, I need to make twelve copies of this letter. I also need to know if you have some paper that can handle some bad weather," Ida asks. The cashier shows Ida some waterproof paper. They have a new copier specifically made to print on the waterproof paper. It sets and stabilizes the print so that it can withstand damp conditions for a long time.

Ida looks the paper over, and agrees to it. The cashier makes the copies, and gives Ida an envelope to put them in. Ida pauses at the end of the counter on her way out. She pulls a notebook and a pen from her purse. She takes each copy and writes something from her notebook on each one. Then she heads home.

In the kitchen, Ida takes one copy and places it into one of the clear containers, the vessels she has specifically chosen for the task. She does this for all twelve containers. She seals the lids as tight as she can, and puts them back into the box they came in. She carries the box to the car, and puts it in the trunk.

It's been a long day, and Ida decides to rest for a bit. As she lies down on the couch, she feels that all is well in the world, and she smiles intently thinking about all the plans she has.

Chapter 14 English Lake

On the next Saturday, Ida, Elisabeth, and Trinity decide to hide their own geocache.

"Where should we go, Grandma?" Elisabeth asks.

"Well, I have been looking, and I scoured the online map. I don't see that there is a cache at the English Lake boat ramp yet," Ida says.

"Where is that?" Elisabeth asks.

"Oh, I know where it is," Trinity says. "It's a drive, but it's nice out, and your grandma needs to get out."

So they drive south down the highway, and turn at a couple of county roads. Finally, they reach the parking lot and the boat launch.

"Good thing no one is here," says Elisabeth. "We can look for a good spot to hide it. I will turn on the GPS on my phone so we can store the location where we hide the cache."

Trinity parks the car, and they get out. Elisabeth starts walking along the edge of the parking lot to look for places to leave the cache.

Trinity stays at the car and waits for the cell phone to get its GPS location.

"I think I am going to walk down to the river to see how the old girl is. It's always been comforting to me to watch the river flow," Ida says.

"Ok, Mom, but don't overdo it. Stay on the path to the water's edge," says Trinity.

"Oh, dear, I will be fine. I was born on the river," Ida says.

"Yeah, but you aren't so young anymore, Mom."

Ida gets her tote bag, and walks down the worn, dirt path. She stands at the water's edge. As she gazes on the sparkling water, she watches a branch float past her. In no time, it is out of sight. "Well, this should be perfect," she says.

She reaches into her bag and pulls out a clear container. She tosses it into the current. One at a time, she pulls out a container, and throws it in the river. The current is brisk, and she watches them float away in no time. She waits a few more minutes, to make sure all the containers are out of sight. Ida smiles widely.

Elisabeth walks up behind her. "It sure is beautiful, Grandma. It's so peaceful down here."

"Yes, it's exactly how I remember it. I could stay down here all day," Ida says.

"Yeah, I could too, Grandma, but Mom is ready to go. We put the cache under a cottonwood tree. Mom took the GPS location to put online," Elisabeth says.

"I can't wait to see who finds it first," says Ida.

"Me, too. Let me help you back to the car," Elisabeth says.

They travel back into town, and go online to make sure their geocache is on the map and ready for someone to look for it. Trinity tells Ida she will make a point of stopping in next week.

"I would like to go to dinner with Elisabeth one day, if that's ok with you," Ida asks.

"That's ok with me. I will tell her to call you," Trinity says. "Bye, Mom."

On Monday, in the afternoon, at what is left of Lomax Station, the owner of the old pumping house is out taking care of his property. Jerry has not owned the historical buildings long, but has become quite fond of them, and the Kankakee River. He makes one last round of securing the old, brick structures, and takes a walk down the gentle slope to the river's edge.

It is a quiet, calm walk down to the water. He enjoys this peacefulness each and every time he comes to Lomax. He brushes through the tall grass, and hears the little creatures that are hiding in it scurry away from him. He gets to the water and takes a moment to pause and gaze upon the beauty of it all. He truly loves this place.

He is looking at the water go by when he sees a strange container bobbing up and down next to the old railroad bridge pier. It looks like it has something in it. He sloshes through the mud along the bank to get to the bottle. He has to hold on to a tree branch to reach out and grab it. Despite a little dirt on it, it looks almost brand new. He rolls it around in his hands to give it a good look. He unscrews the lid and peers inside. There is a piece of paper rolled up in it. It takes a little effort to tighten the paper back up enough to get it out, but he does, and begins to read what is written on it.

"To the finder of this bottle, awaits a great reward. This bottle has been set out in the hope of being found. If you are reading this, then it has been found, and maybe you, the finder, are willing to go a little farther. Please go to www.geojamboree.com and create an account using the name provided in this note. Use the exact name that is printed, and fill out the owner portion with your contact information. A time will come when the journey will come to fruition, and you will be granted a great reward. Please keep the account up to date in order to receive the reward. You have been chosen for this expedition, and may you truly be blessed."

Jerry puts the note back in the bottle. He is very perplexed, but he takes the wet container with him to his car and hurries home.

A few days later, Jerry is looking for some paperwork, and goes to his car in the garage to look. He picks up the pile of papers, and brings them back in the house. As he is thumbing through the pile, he remembers the bottle.

He rushes back out to the car. The container is still there where he left it, on the floor, in the back. He picks it up and brings it back in. He gets the lid opened back up, and the note comes out smoothly this time. He reads the note again. It says to go to www.geojamboree.com and log in with the username.

Jerry powers up his computer and connects to the Internet. He types in the website. Sure enough, there it is. “Hmm, that is interesting,” he says aloud. He reads the home screen and reads it again. It looks legitimate. He is still not sure, so he goes to a search engine to find out more about the website. All the comments are good, but he needs to really know. He goes to the Better Business Bureau site, and he sees that there are no problems and no known issues.

“Well it looks ok, I guess,” he says. “What the heck, I might as well try it. They are not asking for money or anything personal, I guess.” He creates the username just as it says on the note, and fills out the required information. The website says it will send him a confirmation email to finalize the account. He logs into his email address. Sure enough, there it is. He verifies the username by clicking the link to activate it. He reads the note again. It says to keep it secure for future contact, so he stores it in his safe with his other important paperwork. He wonders what it all means, but it sure was fun to find it.

It is shortly after lunch. Ida is sitting in her chair, sorting the mail, when the phone rings. It is within reach, so she picks it up and says hello.

"Yes, Mom? This is Trinity. I was wondering when you want to have Elisabeth over again. She's been asking me. I keep telling her you will call when you're ready, but you know kids."

"Yes, dear, I sure do. How about Monday? I think it's a holiday from school, if I read the calendar right. You know the one you put on my refrigerator?" Ida asks.

"Yeah, you're right. They do have Monday off. I will bring her over on my way to work. See you then," Trinity says.

Chapter 15 Dunn's Bridge

Monday comes so very quickly, but Ida has all her things ready to go for the day. Trinity drops off Elisabeth and sees that Ida has the garage door open to meet her.

"I am ready to go. Are you?" Ida says.

"Oh, yes, Grandma! I am ready to go! I'm glad it finally stopped raining."

"Me, too, dear, but we need that rain so all the plants can grow."

"I know, but I really like the sun," Elisabeth says.

"So do I," Ida says and she turns the key to start the car.

They travel out of town, and to the south. "Where are we going today?" Elisabeth asks.

"I thought we could go to Dunn's Bridge. I saw on the geo site they have a couple of geocaches there to find. It's not really too far. Plus, the bridge is so neat if I remember correctly. I haven't been down there in years," Ida says.

“That sounds cool,” Elisabeth says. “I love seeing the old bridges. I bet you have a story to tell about all of them.”

“There are always good stories to tell about old bridges, especially the ones around here,” Ida says. “The bridge upstream from where we’re going has a very strange story.”

“Tell me!” Elisabeth says.

“It’s an old, county road bridge. I can’t remember any of the names, but the story is about a couple,” and Ida begins the tale.

It was crisp, fall evening, just before dusk. A newlywed couple was traveling north along the gravel county road. It was a majestic ride to see the fall colors, and they were thrilled to be out together enjoying each other’s company. As they drove towards the dense tree line, they could smell the grain in the field, ready to harvest. It was a peaceful quiet that surrounded them. They came to the end of the tree row, just before the bridge. In a lightning instant, a dog ran out of the weeds. The lady saw it first, and grabbed the man’s arm tightly. He saw it too, but it was too late. There was no way to avoid hitting the dog.

He swerved to the right at the same moment the dog made the perilous decision to keep running. The man lost control of the car. The car veered off the road, and picked up speed as soon as it left the roadway. The dog went under! The car kept sliding, through the tall weeds, and toward the field. They finally crashed into some trees with low hanging branches.

He was thrown out of the car near the roadway. It was the next day when another motorist came upon the gruesome scene. He found the man lying in the road, dead.

The authorities came to investigate. They found the dog's body in the weeds, but to their horror, the dog's head was gone! They searched the whole area, but they never found the dog's head or the woman's body.

"For real, Grandma?" Elisabeth asks. "Do you believe that?"

"Yes, that is the story that has been told since the fifties. Supposedly, the woman still roams the area wearing the dog's head, and looking for her husband. The teenagers go there on dares to see who will chicken out first," Ida says.

"That sounds scary. We should go there on Halloween," Elisabeth says.

"Well, I don't know if I can go that far anymore, dear. It's a long walk to get to the bridge. The bridge and the road are both closed, and you have to walk nearly a mile to get there," Ida says.

"Maybe I can dare my friends to go, but I will need to be brave," Elisabeth says.

Elisabeth checks her cell phone to see how close they are getting to the geocache. They are going to look for the one hidden at Dunn's Bridge.

"I know the place well. It's a beautiful sight. It's a pedestrian bridge now, and it has been well kept over the years," Ida says.

Elisabeth reads the description in her geocaching app. "Yeah, it says here it was made out of parts of the Ferris wheel that was at the World's Fair."

"Yes, that is how the story goes, and it makes the bridge look so majestic as soon as you see it," Ida says.

Ida turns off the county road, and drives down the lane toward the access site. When they get close enough, Elisabeth sees the bridge in all its glory.

"I read that it is a steel arch bridge. That is so cool looking. It doesn't look very old," Elisabeth says.

"It still looks like I remember it, after all these years," Ida says.

They park by the boat launch near the bridge. Elisabeth walks up on the bridge deck to look around for clues to where the cache is hiding.

"What do the clues say, dear?" Ida asks.

"This says 'it's a small cache in a safe place.' Some people have found it and wrote 'it's a quick grab and go'," Elisabeth says.

"Well, keep looking. It must not be too obvious, but easy to reach. Look all around the bridge near the river bank. Maybe it's out of sight by the concrete somewhere," Ida says.

Elisabeth searches all around for a few minutes. "I found it!" Elisabeth exclaims. She points to where it is hiding. "It is right here!" She opens it up to see what's inside.

"It's in good shape for being out in the weather. Let's sign the log and leave a game token for the other people," Ida says.

"I put the game piece in and put it right back where I found it," Elisabeth says.

"This is so much fun! I really enjoy finding these," Ida says.

"Well, Grandma, there is another one here, just up the road. See it here on the map?"

"Oh, walk up there and see if you can find it. I will go get the car and drive up there," Ida says. "Wait for me, and don't open it until I get there."

After Elisabeth walks up the road and is out of Ida's sight, Ida goes to the car and opens the trunk. She pulls out her bag, and starts toward the river. When she reaches the water's edge, she takes out the six containers she has left, and places them into the current.

The river grabs them and carries them away in no time. In a minute, they are gone. Ida smiles and walks back up to the car. She puts her bag back in the trunk and drives up the road to find Elisabeth.

"How's it coming, dear?" Ida says.

"It took a while, but I found it, Grandma. It is really small. The only thing inside it is the log."

"How about signing us in, and we can go back home. It's getting late and your mom will be by to pick you up soon," Ida says.

Elisabeth signs the log, and places the cache back in its hiding place. As they drive, they both enjoy the peaceful serenity of the late afternoon, and it seems as though they are back at Ida's house in no time.

The two arrive at Ida's, happy to be home. Ida sits down in her easy chair to rest and wait for Trinity. A few minutes later, they hear Trinity at the door.

"Hello, it looks like you two had a full day," Trinity says.

"Yes, dear, we went out to look for caches and had lots of fun. Elisabeth found both of them," Ida says.

"Oh, that does sound fun, but you know you shouldn't do so much, Mom," Trinity says.

"I know, but it's for my favorite granddaughter."

Elisabeth smiles at Ida. She remembers she must log in their finds before she forgets, and goes to www.geojamboree.com on Ida's computer.

"Oh, I was hoping you would have that on," Trinity says. "I was looking something up the other day and remembered the story you told us about Joseph and his move to Spondon. I was searching for Spondon and this article came up."

"It was about a man who was killed in the streets of Spondon. They never solved the murder. His name was Enoch Stone!" Trinity says.

"Really, Mom? I'm going to look that up," Elisabeth says.

"Yeah, you can look it up if you want. Just do a search on 'Enoch Stone Spondon'," Trinity says.

"Oh yes, dear, I do remember some talk at the family gatherings about a gentleman who was brutally murdered in a town called Spondon. They used to think it was a group of the royal guards that committed the crime. They suspected the royal family still had an edict issued to find the treasure, and a standing order to direct the royal guards to keep up the search. They desperately wanted to return England to its former glory. They wanted be the dominant financial center of the world," Ida says.

"Here it is, Mom, right here. I can't believe it. There is an article about an Enoch Stone, who was murdered in Spondon. It was never solved," Trinity says.

"Oh, really?" Ida says. "I am just so amazed by that internet! I would have never thought to look for that, let alone find it."

"It doesn't say anything about the royal guards, though," Elisabeth says.

"I don't presume that it would," Ida says. "That would give away a clue to the nature of their true mission. The royals want to keep that quiet."

"Maybe that Enoch Stone isn't the same Enoch Stone we are related to," Trinity says. "Well, it's getting late, and Grandma needs to rest up. It's been a long day for her."

"Alright, Mom, I will log out, and we can get going," Elisabeth says.

"It's always good to spend time with you two. Have a safe trip home," Ida says.

"Yeah, thanks Grandma, it was great. I will tell Mom the scary bridge story," Elisabeth says.

They embrace, say goodbye, and Trinity and Elisabeth go back home.

Chapter 16 Dave and Jimmy

It's a normal day. It's warm, sunny, and the river is running quietly past the boat docks. Dave is sitting in his favorite lawn chair enjoying the view. He is deep in thought, and his finger is circling the top of his beer can in the drink holder. The river relaxes him every time he comes out in his backyard.

He watches the birds swoop down and skim the water. Once in a while, they come up with a fish, land in a tree on the opposite bank, and enjoy their reward. The winds are blowing gently from the south, keeping him cool under the sun's hot rays. He is pleasantly content.

One bird sweeps down very low and springs up quickly, dropping something that makes a good sized splash. "Wow, what was that?" Dave says aloud. It couldn't be a fish. He stands up from his chair, and walks over to the pier to look around.

He sees ripples in the water, and where they radiate from, he sees a small bottle. It is a little dirty, and has some weeds stuck to the top of it. "I can reach that, it's not too far," he thinks. He grips the concrete wall with one hand, and stretches his other arm out as far as he can. "Just a little more, a little more, and I can pull it over here," he thinks.

His fingertips just reach one of the weeds, and he tugs gently to get the bottle to move closer to the wall. “Don’t let go, you weed!” he says. The weed obeys, and holds long enough for him to grab the bottle. He pulls it out of the water and carries it into the grass.

“I have you now,” he says. He picks off some more weeds, and wipes the bottle with a towel he has on his chair. He sees that there is something inside of it. He dries off the lid and opens it.

As he cautiously looks in, he sees a note in good shape. He reaches into the bottle, and gently pulls it out. The paper springs open, and he must use both hands to hold it to read what it says. It says the finder will reap a great reward, but the instructions must be followed carefully, and it must be verified on the website.

“Wow, this looks cool!” Dave says. He takes the note to his computer room, and logs into the website like it says. The site asks for some information, but it’s not too personal, so he fills it in, and saves the account.

“Well, at least it’s a fun mystery,” he thinks. “I have lived on this river my whole life, and nothing like this has ever happened to me, so let’s see where it goes.” He realizes he is quite hungry, so he logs off the website, and goes to the kitchen to get some lunch.

The day starts off well, because Jimmy gets the boat motor to start on the first try. "It's going to be a good day," Jimmy thinks. He unties the boat from the mooring, and pushes up the throttle. The motor seems to run very well so far. As he runs the boat upstream, the motor purrs like a smooth sewing machine, and it pushes the boat easily against the current. The boat drives forward over the gentle, flowing river. The water looks crystal clear today.

Jimmy sets the throttle midway, and sits down to watch for any debris floating down the river. It shouldn't take him long to get to the fallen tree. The landowner said it was just a few minutes upstream from Jimmy's house. He figures he can check it out first, and then get a game plan together before he and Dave come back to remove it.

Soon, the tree comes into sight. "Wow, it's a huge one!" Jimmy thinks. "If it looks that big from here, I wonder how big it will be when I get up close to it." He presses on toward the giant tree. As he gets closer, he sees a lot of debris piling up against it. He carefully directs the boat around the canopy end of the tree, and threads his way through. The boat makes it around easily. Jimmy lets off the throttle, and drifts into the piles. From here, he can dislodge some of the branches and see the best way to dismantle the mess. He will get help from Dave to move the larger logs back up to the bank.

He is moving some of the small, dead limbs when a bottle pops up. "Whoa!" he shouts. He stumbles back, thinking it's a muskrat, or even worse, a snake, and nearly falls backward out of the boat. "Whew, almost went swimming there," he says.

The bottle floats silently next to the fallen tree, and bobs up and down with the river current. Jimmy reaches over and grabs it. "Doesn't look bad," he thinks. "It's sealed tight and looks like whatever is in it stayed dry."

He sits down on the boat cushion, and takes a good, long look at the bottle. He opens it up. The smell smacks him in the face immediately. It is a familiar fragrance he remembers from his youth. He realizes it is the comforting scent of his grandmother's perfume. "I'm losing my mind," he thinks. "This river is playing tricks on me."

He squeezes his hand into the bottle and pulls out the note. It says 'you have found a most fantastic vessel. Now you may receive a great reward'. It instructs him what to do next. He must log into a website and verify his find. It says to keep the note in a safe place, as verification of the treasure hunt may take a long time.

Jimmy thinks this is really weird, so he puts the note back in the bottle, and screws the top back on. He finishes the reconnaissance of the logjam, and decides on a plan. He stows the bottle in a cubbyhole to keep it safe on the ride home. He will verify the note when he gets there. He starts the motor, heads downstream, and docks the boat. He gets some supplies ready for the next trip.

He is busy securing the boat when he remembers the bottle. He gets it out of the cubbyhole and takes it in the house with his other stuff. He thinks about telling Dave, but Dave will think he's crazy, and that it's just a silly thing. He decides to wait awhile before he tells. He will go to the website first, and see if anything happens after that.

"Hello, Dave? Can you drive today?" Jimmy asks over the phone. "Sure, you can pick me up in about an hour." Jimmy gets his things together, and finishes his coffee while he waits for Dave. He glances down at the newspaper on the table.

He sees a story about a Florida man who had an uncle that lived here, a long time ago. He is looking for anyone who has information of what happened to him. This guy from Florida used to visit his aunt in the late 1950's, and his uncle was a very good friend to him during the few times he came to visit. When he moved to Florida, he lost contact with them. He was hoping to find out what ever happened to his uncle. The last known lead he had was that the uncle landed in prison somehow, but he vanished without a trace after he was released.

Jimmy reads a little more, and thinks the story is very strange. Why would the man come up north to find someone he barely knew? There must be more to the story. It just didn't make any sense to go through all that to find an uncle he only met a few times.

It must have been a slow news day to feature that story, unless somebody has a hidden agenda behind it all. "I'm going to keep an eye out for that uncle," Jimmy thinks. "I wonder if it has something to do with that bottle I found." He hears Dave honk his truck horn, so he goes out to meet him.

Dave and Jimmy drive into downtown Kankakee for their monthly meeting with the other river caretakers. All the regular members are there, and they discuss their plans to help the river. Dave is talking to Joe about the cleaning project when the LaPorte liaisons walk in.

Jimmy lights up with joy. “Well, great to see you guys here! What a surprise. Hey Dave, look who showed up. What’s going on up in Indiana?” Jimmy says.

Dave turns around and a smile crosses his face. “Hey, good to see you guys. I was hoping you two would come. I have a crazy story to tell you,” Dave says.

“I was out in my lawn chair, you know, watching the river, and enjoying the scenery, when I heard a loud splash. I walk over to the seawall and there’s this bottle floating around. I thought it was nothing at first, but when I got it out of the water, it had a note in it,” Dave says.

“Really, you were just sitting there?” they ask.

“Oh, yes, well you know, taking a break. Anyway, the note in the bottle said to log into this website called geo something,” Dave says.

“No, it’s geojamboree,” Jimmy says.

“Oh, yes, how do you know, Jimmy?” Dave asks.

"Yeah, Jimmy, where you slinking around Dave's house?" they ask.

"Heck, no," Jimmy says. "I found one too."

"Remember when I went to check the logjam up river? I found a bottle with a note in it, too. It said to go to that geojamboree site. It gave me a username, so I logged in. The note said a great reward awaits, and patience is required, or something like that," Jimmy says.

"Yeah," Dave says. "I did the same thing, logged in that name, and then I am supposed to wait. It said to keep it safe, because they will need it for verification before I can collect."

The two liaisons look at Dave and Jimmy like they have really lost it now. "I think you two have been drinking river water," one liaison says.

"Yeah, or some crazy adult beverages," says the other liaison.

"Whatever it is, I'll have what they're having!" the other says.

"No, really you two, we can show you the notes!" Dave says.

“I am not showing them the note. They already think we’re crazy. I will just keep it safe, just in case, you know,” Jimmy says.

“Whoever put the bottles in the river is either doing it for fun, or it might amount to something, and it didn’t cost me a dime,” Dave says.

“Yeah, you’re right. It does sound pretty cool. Let us know what happens,” say the liaisons.

Chapter 17 Butterfly

Trinity wakes on a Thursday morning. While she gets ready for work, she has a strange, sinking feeling in her stomach. She does her morning routine, and makes sure Elisabeth has all her things before leaving for school.

Work goes well all morning, and everything seems in order, but she can't seem to shake the strange feeling. In fact, as the morning goes by, it gets far more poignant. She orders some lunch, but isn't able to finish it. She gets her wallet out to pay for her meal, and finds a crumpled up note in her purse. It is a reminder she wrote down about Ida's doctor appointment. She thinks to herself for a minute. "That's strange. That appointment was a long time ago. I would have thrown that out by now."

She has a feeling that her mom needs something. She has few moments before returning from lunch, so she calls her mom. The phone rings through to Ida's answering machine, and while it's ringing, Trinity gets the feeling that all is not well. In a couple of hours she will be off work and driving home, so she will stop by to check on her mom.

By afternoon, the weather has changed, and the sky looks very strange. When Trinity leaves from work, a growing rain cloud hovers in the south, and it looks ominous at best. As she drives, she notices the sun start to beam out of the west, and it streams through the edge of the cloud in a hazy, mystical way.

The next stoplight turns red, so while she is waiting she grabs her cell to see if she missed Ida's call. She swipes the screen and sees that she is still logged in to the geojamboree website. "That's weird," Trinity thinks. "I haven't been on that site since I went out with Elisabeth and Mom."

The sun's glare gets brighter, so she tilts the phone to get a better view of the display. For an instant, she swears she sees an image of a cross. She blinks her eyes to focus, and looks out of her driver's side window. She blinks and looks again, and sees a rainbow out on the horizon. The biggest, clearest, most colorful rainbow she has ever seen. It starts somewhere north of town and looks like it travels to infinity. The colors are so crisp, and she stares at it so long, she forgets she is at the stoplight.

She hears a horn honk from the car behind her. The light is green, so she proceeds through it, but decides to pull over to see the rainbow once more before it's gone. It is so majestic, she knows she must have a picture of it, so she puts her phone in camera mode, and clicks off a quick photo.

It is at that moment she realizes her mom is all right. She feels a sense of peace flowing over her like water. She puts the car in gear and drives to her mom's.

As Trinity pulls in Ida's driveway, she already knows, and is prepared to accept it. The door is locked, and the house is totally calm and quiet. She can't recall ever being here and not even hearing a bird sing.

She steps in the house, and everything is in order. The answering machine is blinking that it has new messages. She checks the parlor and the sewing room, but is sure she knows what to expect. As she makes her way past the kitchen and down the hall, she can see that the bedroom door is open. She walks in through the open door and sees Ida.

There is her mother, Ida. She looks very peaceful and at one with forever. Trinity is completely overwhelmed and begins weeping. She sits down on the bed next to her mom, and gazes at her loving face. She holds her hand, and begins to pray. She thanks God for blessing the world with her mother's love. She thanks Him for everything good in the world, and promises to help others stay faithful and just, and that they learn to be kind people, as kind as Ida.

After a long, quiet time, Trinity goes out to the parlor and phones 911 to inform them that her mother has passed. As she hangs up the phone, she sees a printout on the computer keyboard. She walks over to see what it is as she waits for the responders to come. It is a color printout of a magnificent butterfly. The caption reads "Butterflies are angels in disguise!"

Trinity stays until the reports are filled out, and all the emergency responders leave. She is given a card from the coroner with whom to contact for the arrangements. After everyone has gone, she checks over the house before she leaves for home. It takes her a moment to actually put the car in gear to pull out of the driveway.

Elisabeth hears Trinity walk in the front door. "Hey, Mom! Dad ordered us a pizza and we saved you some," Elisabeth says.

"Uh, that sounds good. Thank you," Trinity says. Her husband comes down the hallway and sees that she is in a daze.

"Are you all right, Honey?" he asks. "I haven't said anything to Elisabeth, yet."

"I need to tell her," Trinity says, and she fights back the tears.

Trinity gathers herself together, and asks Elisabeth to join her in the living room. Elisabeth can see that something is terribly wrong by the look on her mom's face.

"Elisabeth, life is precious, and we must always enjoy the time we have with the people we love. I don't know how to tell you this, so I will be straight with you. Your Grandma Ida passed away last night in her sleep. She must have been sleeping peacefully when she passed, because she looked so comfortable in her bed," Trinity says.

Elisabeth can feel tears welling up in her eyes. "Oh, Mom, was she sick? I thought she was feeling good. The doctor said she was fine."

"I know, Elisabeth. It's just one of those things we can't understand. When it is our time, we have no choice. We can only hope the memories can carry on through those we love," Trinity says.

Elisabeth is overwhelmed with sadness. She loves her grandma more than anything in the world. She wonders how she will be able to go on without her, she was such a strong woman, and she always made Elisabeth feel loved.

"Grandma made sure we knew the best times of her life," Elisabeth says.

"Yes, she did, and we need to be thankful we had those times with her. Elisabeth, I found this picture by her computer and thought you should have it." Trinity hands Elisabeth the printout of the beautiful butterfly.

Elisabeth lights up, and more tears begin rolling down her cheeks. "Oh, Mom, I sent that to her last night in an email! I found it online when I was doing homework. When I saw it, I thought it was so pretty, and I thought she would like it. I was hoping she would know how to open it. I never expected her to know how to print it!"

"Your grandma was always a quick learner. She sure picked up the Internet fast. It was intuitive for her, despite her age," Trinity says.

"Thank you for bringing this, Mom. I will keep it forever," Elisabeth says.

The coroner informs the family that Ida died of natural causes. She apparently had a severe heart condition. Ida never told anyone because she didn't want anybody to worry. The coroner was surprised it didn't happen sooner, and told Trinity he thought Ida must have been a truly strong woman.

Trinity's brother and sister fly into town to help plan the funeral visitation and the burial. The visitation will be the evening before the funeral, and she will be buried next to her husband in the family plot.

The visitation is very serene. Ida's friends from church and her neighbors are there. Many people come to pay their respects. The next day, after the service, the funeral director asks Trinity if she and Elisabeth would like to have a moment alone with Ida. Trinity sees Elisabeth sitting over by the window, by herself, just staring out into nothing. Trinity goes to her, puts her arm around her, and asks if she would like to say goodbye to Ida in private. Elisabeth looks up at her and says yes.

The room is empty. Elisabeth holds Ida's hand one last time, and whispers to her, "Grandma, thank you for all the time we spent together. I will remember all the stories you told me, and I will carry them forward with honor." Then, Elisabeth reaches into her pocket and pulls out a geocoin. She places it in Ida's hands, and quietly whispers, "I know you found home."

The funeral procession arrives at the cemetery, and Ida is laid to rest. The gathering at the church afterward is lighthearted, the way Ida would have wanted. They trade stories of the good times they had with Ida.

The family returns to Trinity's house. Elisabeth enjoys seeing her mom, her aunt, Diane, and her uncle, John, sitting together again. They all laugh when they remember the days they had growing up, and how enjoyable they were.

Trinity goes into the den and brings out a folder. She opens it up to read the letter inside. "I got this yesterday," she says. "It is from Mom's attorney. He wants to set up a time to meet, as soon as possible, to go over her will. I know we all have things to get back to, but the attorney can meet us tomorrow."

"Well, that's fine with me. I could make a meeting tomorrow," John says.

"I can make it, too," Diane says.

"All right, we will meet at his office tomorrow. I will call him first thing in the morning," Trinity says.

Chapter 18 Will

The next day, Trinity, John, and Diane meet at the attorney's office.

"Good morning. I'm glad to see everyone could make it. Ida gave me her will, and her wishes are very clear," the attorney says. "She wants all of her personal effects, including her house, to be divided equally among her children. Additionally, each person is to receive $275,000 from her savings account. She wanted each of you to know she loved you very much, and will always look over you. It's pretty simple, and I will finalize all the formalities if you'd like."

They agree to let the attorney handle it. "Then if there isn't anything you have questions about, I think that covers it," the attorney says.

They thank him for all the help he has given Ida over the years, and they prepare to leave. Elisabeth is in the reception foyer, putting on her coat, when the attorney remembers he needs to speak with her for a moment in private.

He and Elisabeth return to his office. He hands her a note, a key, and a small necklace.

"Ida gave me this key, it's to a safe deposit box, and I was instructed to give it to you if she was unable to do it herself. The box is at the bank downtown. It's been paid for through the will for as long as you need it. If you would like me to accompany you to the bank, I can do that, but you can go alone, if you wish. Please keep it safe. You are listed on the access card, but you will need to show identification. Elisabeth, your grandma was quite a special person. I will remember her fondly. If you need anything at all, let me know," the attorney says.

"Thank you very much," says Elisabeth, and she returns to the foyer to find her mom.

"There you are. I was wondering where you went," Trinity says.

"The attorney gave me something from Grandma. It was in her will. Look, it was this necklace," Elisabeth says. She holds the necklace out to show her mom.

"Oh, that was her favorite necklace! You deserve to have it."

Alone in his office, the attorney shuttles his chair across the plastic chair pad, and to a filing cabinet next to his desk. He shuffles through the cabinet, to put Ida's file back in its place. He glances over, and sees an envelope sitting on top of her file that he doesn't remember seeing before. He wonders when she could have brought it. Maybe she brought it the last time she was here discussing her will.

He picks it up, and it is heavy. He grabs his letter opener. As he cuts open the top, a key drops out and lands on the floor. It looks just like the key he gave to Elisabeth, but when he looks at it closely, he notices the box number is different.

He looks in the envelope and finds a letter from Ida, addressed to him, with a list of instructions. She must have brought this the last time she was here, he thinks. The letter tells him to take the key, remove the information from the safe deposit box, and follow that set of instructions very carefully.

He remembers Ida well, and it is no surprise to him that she has pulled one last rabbit out of her hat. She enjoyed doing that to him over the years, and she was very good at it.

A few days later, he goes to the bank. The vault attendant looks at the key, and pulls up the signature card to verify his access. She asks to see the attorney's identification. After she is satisfied that he is who he says he is, she leads him to the vault.

Once in the vault, she uses her master key, while he turns his key, to release the box. She leads him to the booth so he can look through the contents in private. He thanks her and closes the door.

He opens the safe deposit box. Inside, he finds another of Ida's notes. This one instructs him to telephone an agent at Lloyd's of London to set up an account. He is to set this up to finalize her wishes, now that she has passed on. The name, telephone number, and email address of the agent are given. There is also a bank account number.

He has to read this part of the note a few times to be sure he is reading it correctly. Ida has left an account with a balance of very substantial proportion! He is truly amazed at the amount. He never knew she was that well off.

Ida has set up and left him detailed instructions of a system consisting of twelve notes. Each note is to be used to verify the finder of its companion note, using the specified username and password. Any finder of a note was instructed to go to a website and enter their contact information.

The insurance agent is to use a portion of the fund, as approved by him, Ida's attorney, to verify the legitimacy of the finders. However, he, Ida's children, and Elisabeth, have the final approval in determining the authenticity of the finders.

The instructions also state that the system is to be brought into action only after six or more of the notes have been found and logged in by a finder.

He finds one last envelope in the box. It is sealed, but the instructions written on the outside say it is to be given to the insurance agent, for his use only, to fulfill the final steps for each finder.

Ida's attorney is dumbfounded. "Wow, I can't believe she has done all of this on her own, and just in the these last few weeks. There are some things I don't understand, but she has entrusted me to take care of this, and I will honor her last wishes," he thinks.

He puts the documents in his briefcase, and closes the box. He thanks the vault attendant, and proceeds to the teller to verify Ida's bank account.

"Yes, Sir, how may I help you?" asks the teller.

“Well, I have this account number, and I need to know two things. What is the current balance, and am I the designated signatory on the account?” the attorney asks.

“I will need to see your identification, please, before I can inform you of your access rights,” the teller says.

He hands her his identification, and she checks the account. “Yes, Sir, you are on the account. Let me get the balance for you,” the teller says. She switches screens, and a strange look comes over her. She switches screens again to bring up the verification once more. “It looks like that is the correct amount,” the teller says. She prints out a small receipt and hands it to him.

“That is the balance as of today, Sir. Have a great day, and if you need anything at all, please don’t hesitate to ask anyone here. We can help you with anything you may need,” she says.

He takes the receipt and walks away. “That was weird,” he thinks. As he gets to the door, he takes a look at the receipt. He stops dead in his tracks. “There has to be a mistake. This is far greater than the account balance listed on the instruction sheet,” he thinks.

He turns around to go back to the teller. She knows exactly why he is coming back. He gets to the counter and asks, “Is this right?”

“Yes, Sir, I verified it three times to be sure. You seem perplexed.”

“Well, it is much greater than what I was expecting. It is much more than what is on this sheet,” the attorney says.

“Sir, those are the correct number of zeroes. The account balance sheet you have is older, and doesn’t show any updates,” the teller says.

“Well, thank you, then. It has been quite an interesting day,” he says.

“Yes, for both of us,” she says and smiles. “Have a wonderful day, Sir.”

Chapter 19 Honor

Elisabeth is walking home from school on a very sunny day. She starts digging through her backpack to get her sunglasses. As she is searching, she feels something sharp poke her fingers. She grabs the object and pulls it out. It's the key she got from the attorney.

"Oh, yeah, I forgot I put that in there," she thinks. "Well, today is just as good as any. I can do my homework later."

She changes direction and heads toward the bank. She doesn't go to the bank very often, so she doesn't know what to do. When she enters the lobby, she sees a sign, and follows the arrows to where she thinks the safe deposit boxes are.

"May I help you, dear?" asks a teller. The teller reminds Elisabeth of her Grandma Ida. She misses her terribly, and is afraid she may burst into tears now.

"Yes, I think so. I need to see the box that this key goes to," Elisabeth says.

"Let me see the key to get the box number, and I will pull up the security card for verification.

Do you have any kind of identification card with you, dear?" asks the teller.

"Yes, I have this one my mom got for me."

The teller cross checks Elisabeth's card with the box information. "It all looks in order. Let me show you to the vault," the teller says, and takes Elisabeth to the vault. She introduces her to the attendant. "She will take care of you from here, dear," the teller says.

"Hello, there. I have a key for one lock and you have the other. You need to put your key in at the same time I put mine in, and we will unlock the box together. Are you ready?" asks the attendant.

"Yes, I'm ready," Elisabeth says. Elisabeth is thinking this feels really official and she wonders what her grandma has left for her in that box. The box unlocks smoothly, and slides out. The attendant takes Elisabeth to a booth and closes the door. Elisabeth is in the room alone, and she suddenly feels very grown up. She knows she must gather her strength to carry on with whatever her grandma will want her to do.

Elisabeth opens the box. Inside, she finds a note written in Ida's handwriting, and addressed to her. She tilts the box toward the light to make sure she isn't missing anything when she sees something stuck in the back. She puts her hand in and pulls out something very soft. It's a leather pouch.

Her mind begins to race. It speeds back through all the stories that Ida told her. "A leather pouch? Could it be the same one? That just couldn't be possible!" she thinks.

She opens the note from her grandma and begins to read.

"My Dear Elisabeth,

This pouch and its contents are to be held in the greatest confidence. Its existence cannot be divulged to anyone. The box you found it in has been set up to hold its contents for as long as you wish. The pouch contains a coin. This coin has brought great financial fortune to our family throughout the years. It is only to be used for positive things! You will see that this coin bears the likeness of Caesar. It is now entrusted to you. You are capable of keeping it in good faith. The pouch also contains a length of string. The string was used during biblical times in a typical carpenter's livelihood. Please keep both of them safe and secure. They are best left in meager, humble hands, and are never to be let into the hands of the greedy. The true power of these objects cannot be known by any human, and should be revered in great honor. I believe in you, Elisabeth, and your ability to honor those who have gone before you. Matthew 22:21.

Your Grandma and Friend in the Lord, Ida"

Elisabeth can feel the gravity of the note, and all that has been entrusted to her. She takes a moment and prays to God for guidance. She also whispers softly to Ida, and asks her for her help in fulfilling her wishes.

She carefully places the note and the pouch back into the box, and exits the booth. She sees the vault attendant and waves her over.

"I'm ready to put it back now," Elisabeth says. They both put their keys in, and lock the box securely.

"Do you have any questions?" the attendant asks.

"How much does it cost to keep this safe deposit box open here?" Elisabeth asks.

"We can check that, just come with me to the terminal," the attendant says. She logs into the system, and brings up the box number. "Hmmm," she says. "This is strange. It says here this box is set up on auto renewal. The account it is attached to is set up to renew indefinitely," the attendant says.

"How long is that?" Elisabeth asks.

"Well, longer than both our lives combined times one hundred. So it looks like there is nothing you have to do. The box is here for you as long as you want it," says the attendant.

"Oh, cool, thank you so much. You've been very helpful," Elisabeth says, and she tucks the key back inside her backpack. She has to get home before dinner.

Chapter 20 Jude

It's 9:30 in the morning. Ida's attorney, Jude, is going through his files on top of his desk from the last few days. As he picks one up, he sees a note stuck to the front of it. The note says, "Call Lloyd's, Ida." He almost forgot! He was supposed to call the insurance broker in London, to set up the account for Ida's will.

He spins his chair around too quickly, and bumps the computer mouse off to the side. The screen saver disappears, but the cursor is still positioned over the browser window. He opens it, searches for the insurance agent, and gets the link. He locates the company directory, and scans the names. The highlighted name of the new accounts manager catches his eye. "Well, Matthew seems like a good, honest name. Matt it is," he thinks.

He clicks the email link, and sends a message to Matthew to inquire about setting up a new account for his client. Satisfied that his email was sent successfully, he goes back to sorting the files on his desk. Within a few minutes, he sees the new message alert. "Oh good, it looks like someone is getting back with me already," Jude thinks, and opens the email.

"Hi, my name is Matthew, and I read your request. It looks like you will need a special services account. We would be happy to assist you in setting it up, and we will host it until you complete your business. Please call the following number. Sincerely, Matthew, New Accounts Manager, Lloyd's."

Jude picks up the phone and calls the number. After a few rings, a voice answers.

"Hello, this is Matthew. How may I assist you?"

"Hello, Matthew. My name is Jude. I just got your email about the new account I need to set up."

"Oh, yes, I would be happy to assist you, Jude. I see you need a special account with possible long term settings. We can accomplish that for you. What are the parameters that you require?" Matthew asks.

"I will need two financial accounts, one designated as the finder disbursement portion account, and the other for the verification control group. In the disbursement account, I will need to have several transactions set up after verification of each person, and all appropriate fees or taxes taken care of, based on their residency," Jude says.

"That's not a problem. We can do that," Matthew says.

"Then, I will also need an account set up for all fees relating to the implementation of the directions. Can you prepare a fee schedule contract, so I know how much the estate could be expending to implement the directions?" Jude asks.

"Absolutely," Matthew says.

"Can the contract be set up in a long term fee structure using 5 years, 10 years, 20 years, and 50 years?" Jude asks.

"Yes, we can set those rates based on those increments. How many instances are we anticipating?" asks Matthew.

"Well, let's see, the directions call for a possible twelve finds, with a minimum of six finds. So, let's say we should be prepared for twelve. Each find will have to have verification. The parameters for the verification must include background checks, all online search reviews, court record searches, private investigator reports, and potential interviews with or without independent legal counsel. Now, these finders could come from anywhere in the world, so we should budget for that," Jude says.

"I can illustrate the typical cost incurred to fulfill each requirement, and insert it into the contract. Our standard overhead charge is 30% if completed in the first 3 years, 50% for years 3 through 10, and 60% for every year after that, up to a maximum of 75 years. At that time, Lloyd's must revisit the contract," Matthew says.

"That sounds great. I can't stress enough the importance of clearly spelling out the details of the contract. We must make sure the basic intent of the directions is fulfilled," Jude says.

"All right then, Sir. I will get right on it. I have to say, I have written a lot of contracts, but none of this nature. I'm not saying I can't do it, I am just saying this is not of the ordinary. We do have a couple of agents who are familiar with this type of request, so I will have them review it before I send it to you," Matthew says.

"Very good then, Matthew. When you get those contracts prepared, please email them to me. Then I will set up the transfer," Jude says.

“Yes, and thank you very much. I’m confident we will get this set up to your satisfaction and the needed outcome,” Matthew says.

Jude hangs up the phone, without worry. He feels that Matthew and his company can handle this. He makes a few more notes, and places Ida’s file securely back in its proper place in the cabinet.

Chapter 21 Matthew

A few years have passed since Matthew last spoke with Jude, the American attorney. Matthew has been busily working his way up the corporate ladder. He is proud of the fact that he has many more contracts in his portfolio now.

He has become the most sought after agent in the firm, and has diligently helped all sorts of clients get through tough times. He has garnered a large, corner office that overlooks a spectacular park. He spends most of his time following up on contracts, making sure they are in force, and helping his clients achieve their financial goals.

His investing acumen at picking the right point of entry and exit has gained the trust of his best clients. He has filled his portfolio with the maximum allowed for any agent.

As he is sitting at his desk one afternoon, looking at one of several computer monitors, he refreshes the display to his far right. He sees that he needs to pay close attention to a trade he entered into a few weeks ago.

He quickly logs in to the account just in case he needs to adjust his stop order if the shares start trending lower. Indeed, as he is watching, the ticker steadily moves downward. He watches intently as it flirts with his stop price, but it seems today is not the day that it will break it. He relaxes a bit and turns his attention to the other running programs.

On his larger, center display, an icon is flashing, and it catches his eye immediately. He begins to wonder what account it is for, because it's an icon that he hasn't used in years. He typically assigns certain icons of a specific design to the special accounts, but this one isn't jogging his memory.

He hesitates for a second, moves his mouse over it, and clicks on it. It opens immediately and fills the entire display. It is a login page for a website. He is very disappointed with himself because he has absolutely no idea what the website is for.

The page is prompting him to enter his username and password. "Oh, I have a bad feeling about this. It could be a virus. Maybe it's an old account I set up a long time ago, and I didn't complete the final run. Either way, this is bad, because I must have set up this account, and I don't remember the username and password. I could be locked out, and not be able to finish the client's request! Maybe I set up an alert that emailed me a reminder when it reached its end run," he thinks.

Desperately, Matthew logs into his email account. He is quite dismayed, because he doesn't see any alerts or messages that relate to the mystery account.

"Nothing! Nothing at all! I am in deep here," he thinks. "Wait a minute. This email account was set up when there was a changeover in corporate hosting. The old one was closed two years ago. There's been no incoming email from it. I will call IT to see if the old account is still accessible, then I can search it for any messages that may be there that I didn't receive."

"Hello, IT support, how can I help you?" a soothing female voice says.

"Hello there. I have an unknown account showing up on my screen. I think I may have sent the account information to myself through the old corporate account. Is there any way to access the old email account server and forward those messages to my new email address?" Matthew asks.

"Well, let's see, Sir, give me a minute."

Matthew can hear the sound of the IT technician typing on her keyboard. In a few seconds, her computer comes back with all the old email server paths.

"Sir, I'm sorry to say that the old server for those email accounts was terminated two years ago. After one year, the legacy paths are no longer supported, so all messages sent or received from that server would be bounced back as undeliverable. I'm sorry about that," the technician says.

"Oh, that's just great! Look, this is very important. Is there any other way we can retrieve those messages?" Matthew asks.

The technician senses the panic in Matthew's voice. She thinks for a second.

"The archived tapes were stored on another server when we transferred and upgraded the data sets," she says.

"And would the archived backup contain the email account .pst files?" Matthew asks.

"Yes, Sir, they sure would. Was your email login the same as it is now?"

"Yes, it is the same. I haven't changed it since I started," Matthew says.

"Let me see if I can drill down within that server, and locate the oldest .pst file. I will call you back in a few minutes to tell you what I found. Do you have a name I can search for in the email archives if I find something?" she asks.

"Yes, the subject line or the body of the email would contain the name 'Ida'," Matthew says.

"I will get right on it," she says.

With much relief, Matthew thanks the technician. He gets himself a glass of water, and waits patiently for her return call.

The IT technician is able to locate the .pst files in the server. She finds them within an old folder named Matthew. It is a large, but it opens without any errors. She transfers the folder over to her virtual terminal on her system, and restores the .pst file within the current email system directory. It opens with a plethora of old email.

"So far, so good," she thinks. She enters the name "Ida" in the search bar, and the computer begins the search through the file. It only takes a few seconds before three emails pop up that contain the word "Ida". Thinking this must be what he is looking for, she copies the messages that she has found to her system account, and forwards them to Matthew.

Matthew is reviewing another trade to make sure the price doesn't fall below his stop order when his phone rings and his computer beeps simultaneously. He picks up his phone and looks at the display that shows his email inbox.

"Hello, Matthew, I just emailed you three email messages I found on the old server. Two were from your inbox, and one was from your sent items folder," the technician says.

"Oh, yes! I see them! You are unbelievable! The one in the sent items folder is the one I needed. Thank you so very much! You are a lifesaver!"

"No problem, Sir. I'm just doing my job. Don't forget us moles down here when the budget comes up in your executive meetings," she says.

"I assure you, I won't. This is a game changer for the firm, believe me. I will see to it that you receive special recognition for helping me today," Matthew says.

"Thank you. I appreciate that," she says.

Matthew goes back to the mystery website and the login page. He enters the username and password successfully. The system verifies the settings, and opens a startup page.

It has information on it with a few usernames and their account settings. He still doesn't completely remember the details of this account. He looks at the preferences to see if they show the owner's information, because he could cross reference that to his files. He is able to see some information, so he copies and pastes it to his account retriever program. He crosses his fingers.

It comes up with one match! He looks at the name on the account.

"Oh, now I remember! Boy, how could I forget this one? It was the most interesting account I ever had, but I never expected it would be finalized, or even reach its set strike point," he thinks.

He looks carefully through the account information and finds a .pdf file stored within it. When he opens the file, he finds a lengthy set of instructions. He pulls up his chair to get comfortable, and begins to read.

"Yes, I can follow this process. Yes, I can," Matthew says.

Chapter 22 RSVP

It's Saturday morning, and the phone rings loudly. Trinity is sitting at the kitchen counter, drinking her coffee. She picks up the phone.

"Hello?" Trinity asks.

"Hello. Is this Ida's daughter, Trinity?" a strange voice asks.

"Yes, it is. Who is this?"

"My name is Matthew. I am calling from Lloyd's of London. I have had an account established by your mom that has been in existence for years now. It has specific instructions that say to contact you when its parameters were met. I have just reviewed the account, so that's why I am contacting you today," Matthew says.

"I don't understand. I don't know anything about an account," Trinity says.

"Well, let me try to explain. This account names you as a verifier for a system that was set up," Matthew says.

"So you need me to verify something?" Trinity asks. "I'm not sure I'm following you. What system?"

"It's a little difficult to explain. The instructions are directing me to get transportation and anything you may need, because you are to come here to the Lloyd's of London Headquarters in London. You are one of the individuals that must meet here to verify the legitimacy of the contracts," Matthew says.

"This sounds too strange. You just call me out of nowhere, and expect me to believe you?" Trinity asks.

"Yes, Trinity, I understand why you would be suspicious. I will give you all my contact information so you can go online and check. When you get the phone number for Lloyd's of London, please call it, and confirm the legitimacy of my invitation," Matthew says.

"Yes, you can be sure I will be doing that," Trinity says.

"I hope to hear back from you soon. Thank you for speaking with me today," Matthew says.

Trinity is very leery of the caller, but she is curious, too. She opens her laptop, researches the contact, and finds a general number for Lloyd's.

"Well, it's worth a try, I guess," she says.

She dials the number. An operator with the same British accent as Matthew's greets her.

"Lloyd's of London. How may I direct your call?" the voice asks.

Trinity tells the operator the information Matthew gave her. The operator confirms it to be true and correct, and offers to transfer her. Trinity waits while she is transferred to another line. The same voice that called her this morning answers.

"Hello, this is Matthew."

Trinity is so relieved that this wasn't a prank. "Hi Matthew, this is Trinity."

"Well, hello. I am so glad you called back," Matthew says. He opens the file that contains the specifications that he must relay to her.

"These are the requirements according to Ida's instructions. I need your information to send you transportation tickets, and all the lodging information for your trip. I will send you an overnight package that contains all the details," Matthew says.

"All right. Is the trip just for me? Am I to come alone?" Trinity asks.

"Yes, you are to arrive here alone."

"I will wait for the itinerary, then. Thank you, Matthew," Trinity says.

"I will be in touch. I have to say, even though I never met her, your mom sure was an interesting woman, wasn't she?" Matthew asks.

"Yes, she was. Goodbye," Trinity says.

Matthew continues down the list, and contacts Elisabeth next. Then he phones Trinity's sister, brother, and Ida's attorney, Jude. He informs each of them of the trip they are to make, with all expenses paid entirely. They will even be given some spending cash to enjoy their time in London.

"That went quite well," Matthew thinks. "Now I need to follow up with the logged in users, get them here, and complete the verification process." He brings up the username screen and starts with the first one in the list, a man by the name of Jerry.

Matthew needs to see if Jerry's email address is still active, so he clicks on the email link and sends a query. He wonders if Jerry will respond to his message and get back to him. Matthew repeats this procedure for each username that has logged in, to see how many reply to his email.

He sees the dates of the logs, and it has been years since some of them logged in. To Matthew's surprise, it only takes a few hours, and the first one responds. He checks the list, and it's the last person who logged in on the website.

"Hello," the email reads. "I was very curious about the legitimacy of the note I found. You know the odds of something like this becoming true. I hope to hear more about the reward. Thanks, Edward."

Matthew hits the reply button, and sends a message back to Edward. He instructs him to check the contact information at his earliest convenience, and to call him at the agency. Edward eagerly replies to Matthew that he will do so very soon.

Matthew is very anxious to get to the office the next day to see if he has received any more replies. When he checks his email account, he sees that there are three more responses! He sends each of them the same contact information, and instructs them to get in touch with him by phone. Within a few days, he has spoken with each of them, and they are all in wonder that he is sending them everything they will need to come to London.

There are still three more he hasn't been able to contact. "Looks like I will have to find them the hard way," he thinks.

He picks up the phone, and contacts the investigative service branch of the firm. He asks them to expedite the search process, since time is of the utmost concern.

Luckily, each investigation only takes a day. He is supplied with a list of the individuals he needs to find. Matthew receives a reply from each of the three people. Like the others, he explains to them the nature of his call, and they are all very pleased with the news that they will be flown to London.

Matthew's day is nearly complete, and he closes down the programs for the evening. He anticipates another sleepless night, because his mind can't rest with all the excitement. Very soon, the finders will be arriving in London for the finalization of the reward disbursement.

Chapter 23 Adventure

It is late in the afternoon on Friday. Trinity disembarks her plane in New York. She checks her ticket and sees she needs to get to Gate 1401. Her flight to London departs in about twenty minutes.

She is walking briskly to the gate when she hears a familiar voice calling from several feet away.

"Hey! Mom! Mom! Over here!"

She turns toward the voice to look at who is yelling, and she sees Elisabeth.

"Elisabeth! What in the world are you doing here?" Trinity asks.

Trinity drops her bag down and gives Elisabeth a great, big hug.

"Oh, wow! Mom, I never expected to see you here," Elisabeth says. "What are you doing here? Where are you going?"

"I am going to London. I am supposed to meet a man at Lloyd's to talk about something Grandma had going on," Trinity says.

"Oh, my! Me too! We must be meeting the same person. I guess we are on the same flight," Elisabeth says.

"Yes, we probably are. Do you know who else is going? Did anyone say?" Trinity asks.

"Nope, all I know is everything is taken care of. It is so strange, but at least it will be interesting to find out what is happening," Elisabeth says.

"Yes, it will be quite the adventure. I'm so glad you are here with me," Trinity says.

They board the plane together, and begin their flight to London. After they land, they are greeted by a limo driver, and taken to a hotel the likes of which they've never seen.

"It is so beautiful. This place is amazing. We get to stay here as long as we want?" Elisabeth asks.

"Yes, and it's all paid for. What fun we will have," Trinity says.

"Don't forget, we do have to meet at Lloyd's in two days, so I guess it's not a free for all," Elisabeth says.

"But, we can have some fun, before and after."

"Yes, Mom, this will be a good time. I wonder what Grandma has in store for us," Elisabeth says.

"She always did have a wonderful sense of adventure, even when I was young," Trinity says.

"Are you ready to go crazy?" Elisabeth asks

"Let's go!" Trinity says.

They hit the town and enjoy some shopping at the most famous stores in London. Then they stuff themselves on authentic fish and chips. Two days go by in a blink, and the morning of the meeting arrives quickly. They meet in the lobby, and find that a limousine is waiting for them in the porte-cochere.

"How cool is this?" Elisabeth asks.

"This will surely be an experience we will remember for the rest of our lives, and we have Grandma to thank," Trinity says.

They climb in the limo as gracefully as they can. They are feeling like superstars. It takes them to the world headquarters of Lloyd's of London. When they arrive, they both look up at the most unusual building they have ever seen. It is architecturally the most distinctive front entrance ever designed.

"This is grander than I would have ever thought. How impressive this is!" Trinity says.

"It is quite beautiful! Well, let's go in and see what Grandma was up to," Elisabeth says.

They walk slowly, to take it all in, and eventually get to the front reception desk. The receptionist saw the limo, and already knows why they are here.

"Hello," the receptionist says. "I presume you are here for the verification meeting?"

"Yes, we are. We are supposed to meet someone named Matthew," Trinity says. She hands the receptionist a card with his name on it.

"He is already in the main board room. Please take the elevator up. When you exit, just go straight toward the oak doors. Have a pleasant day," the receptionist says.

"Thank you. We hope to," Trinity says.

They go to the elevator, and wait for the doors to open. When they get in, Elisabeth whispers to Trinity, "Do you know what floor the board room is on?"

"No, she didn't say."

They look at the panel inside the elevator. "I think it must be this one," Trinity says and pushes the call button labeled Executive Board Room.

The elevator moves quickly and silently, and stops gently on their floor. The pleasing tone of the bell chimes, and the door opens. When they step out, they see an elaborate set of oak doors, ten feet in height, at the end of the hall.

The soft carpeting muffles their footsteps as they walk toward the massive doors. Trinity pulls on the highly polished door handle, and finds that it opens with ease. It is perfectly weighted to swing open with the slightest effort.

"Well, here we go," Elisabeth says, and they walk in.

The room is extremely large. The ceilings are twenty feet high. The walls are paneled in the finest wood, and oiled to a perfect sheen. The smell of the room is heavy with the scent of old mahogany. One moment in this grand room is both intoxicating and humbling.

"Well, I see you made it. Welcome," Matthew says. Trinity sees Matthew enter the room from a hidden paneled door near the head of the table.

"Hello, I am Trinity. This is my daughter, Elisabeth."

"Yes, pleased to meet you. I am Matthew. I am glad you're here. I hope you're having a great time in London, so far."

"Oh, yes! It's been quite wonderful," Trinity says.

"The others have not arrived as of yet, but please, have a seat and make yourself comfortable. They should be here momentarily. Would you like anything? We have all sorts of tea, and several kinds of crumpets. Oh, I mean, would you like some coffee, soda, or snacks, as you Americans say?"

Trinity laughs and tells Matthew they are fine for now.

"Then, I will have the concierge bring some later. Please excuse me, I will be right back. If you need anything, just tap on this door and someone will get you whatever you need," Matthew says.

Trinity and Elisabeth thank him and sit down at the table. Elisabeth is looking around the room.

"Mom, this table is bigger than anything I have ever seen! It looks like it was made from one piece of wood."

"That must have come from a very old tree from long ago, judging by the size of it."

"Do you notice there are only seven chairs around the table?" Elisabeth asks.

"Yes, that is weird, but I am sure we will see why very soon," Trinity says.

The massive door swings open, and Trinity's brother and sister come in. To their great surprise, they are together, in this room, and are overwhelmed with interest of what Ida has planned.

They sit together for a while, and talk about all the good times they had growing up. They summon the concierge, and have some soda and snacks while they wait. They are in the midst of a great story when the paneled side door opens. Ida's attorney, Jude, walks in to greet them.

"Hello, all. It's good to see you made it safely. Ida would be proud to see you all here together. I guess you are wondering just why you're here? Let me start off by saying this whole journey was set up by Ida before she passed. It was not in her will, but I found out about it later. I came across a safe deposit box key that she left within her documents in my office. The instructions were very clear about who was to be present today," Jude says.

Jude sits down at the table and continues. "I set up this account here with Matthew years ago. I wasn't really sure if this meeting would ever take place, but here we are. Ida's instructions were to have you four, and myself, meet here to finalize a verification process. She set up a treasure hunt of sorts, before she passed away."

Matthew comes in the room, greets everyone, and takes a seat next to Jude.

"Please explain the details to them, Jude," Matthew says.

"It seems that Ida set out several bottles, with each containing a message. She gave us these instructions to follow. We are required to interview each person who claims to be a finder of one of the bottles. We are to check each unique message from the bottle that was found, and verify its authenticity. We are to listen to each person's story of how they came about finding the bottle. Then we vote. We vote on whether we think they are being truthful and that their message is legitimate. The instructions require the vote to be an agreement of the majority, but not necessarily a unanimous vote. So, it must be at least three out of five who will verify each finder's legitimacy. After we have made the decision, we will all be given the chance to stay in London for three more days. All of the expenses will be paid, along with a generous spending limit, from an account provided by Ida. Does everyone understand these instructions?"

Not one person says a word. They just shake their heads that they understand the instructions. Everyone is stunned at the news about this whole adventure.

"If everyone has a full understanding of what is to happen, I will let Matthew take over from here," Jude says.

Chapter 24 Finders

Matthew rises from his chair, and proceeds to walk around the room. He turns to the group seated at the table. All eyes are on him, waiting intently for more.

"Thank you for your explanation, Jude," Matthew says. "I have a list of seven finders. Now, first of all, here is the list Jude gave me when he first contacted me. It has the usernames and passwords Ida set up for the seven notes in the bottles. You will find, in front of you, a packet. The first page is a picture of the bottles she used to put the notes in. The second page is the list of usernames and passwords that she used in the notes. The next stack of folders is the dossiers on the people who have come forward at this time. We have done extensive background checks on these people. You will see the findings in each person's file. I will bring each person into this room, and you can ask them anything you want to know. Before they are brought in, I will go over each one before I introduce them. After they leave, I can try to answer any other questions you have about anything contained in their packet. Then you will need to decide on the verification of each one of them. You should consider the fact that each finder is unique. Do not let other finder's information impact your opinion of any other finder. Do you have any questions before we start?"

"Yes, Matthew, do we decide on what they get for finding the notes?" John asks.

"No, you will not. That has already been established in Ida's instructions," Matthew says.

"So, you said there are only seven finders here today. Will there be others?" Trinity asks.

"There could be, but the instructions are very clear that after half of the finders logged in, I was supposed to call this meeting. Anyone else have questions?" Matthew asks. "Then, off we go."

"The first person is a man by the name of Jerry. He is a real estate agent out of Chicago. He found the bottle with the note at a place called Lomax. He is in possession of the original note and the bottle it was found in. The note has been checked and is one that Ida sent out. He logged in with the username and password just a few days after the bottle was placed in the river. His story makes sense because he was the closest to the place where Ida released them. His background check has no red flags. He is a unique character, and seems to know a lot about this place called Lomax. He is like most of the other finders in that he is someone who really enjoys the river and all its history. Does anyone have any questions before I bring him in?" Matthew asks.

The group is flipping through the pages in Jerry's file, but no one speaks up. Matthew nods his head at Jude, who is waiting by the paneled door.

Jerry walks in ands sits down in the empty chair at the head of the conference table.

"Hello, Jerry, these people are here to verify your finding of the note in the bottle. This is not a legal hearing or in any way connected to any judicial branch of any country. This is a private program set up by a private individual. Please speak truthfully and just tell them about how you found the note," Matthew says.

"Uh, well, it was a quiet afternoon, and I was walking the property to make sure everything was secure before I left for the day. Like I always do, I took a walk down to the river. The river has an old railroad crossing bridge next to the property. I was looking in that direction when something caught my eye. I saw this thing bobbing up and down in the water. It was stuck up against the railroad bridge piling. I got to it and was barely able to reach over to get it. When I opened it up, it had instructions. It said that whoever found it was supposed to document that they found it. Well, it wasn't until a few days later that I remembered the note, so I went to the website and did what it said to do. I thought it was really strange, but it was kind of fun to think about what might happen. I am older than all of you, but I can still remember the stories my grandfather used to tell me about putting a message in a bottle. I never thought it would happen to me, so I was up for the game. There is not much else to tell, but I want to thank whoever is responsible for this adventure. I've never been to London before. I haven't had to pay for a thing, and everyone has treated me so well. It's like a magical gift or winning the lottery!"

"Thank you, Jerry. Does anyone have any questions for him?" Matthew asks.

They are all just sitting there, staring at Jerry, and shaking their heads no. Jude leads Jerry out the paneled door.

Finally, Elisabeth speaks up timidly. "I, I think he is legitimate. I believe him."

"Yes, I believe him, too," John says.

"So do I," Trinity says.

“If you are all in agreement, then it is unanimous,” Matthew says. He moves Jerry’s file off to the side, and picks up the next one.

“The second person is a man named Dave. He is from a small town in Illinois, just west of the Indiana State Line. He found the bottle while he was relaxing by the river one afternoon. Dave is retired, and has lived by the river his whole life. He logged the username a few weeks after Ida set the bottles afloat. His story sounds believable, and his background check is on the up and up. Does anyone have any questions about his file before I bring him in?” Matthew asks.

They all look up, and shake their heads. Jude leads Dave into the room and shows him to his chair.

“Please, make yourself comfortable, Dave. The people sitting here are the ones who need to hear your story of how you found the bottle and the note inside of it. Please do not feel intimidated. They are just normal people like you and me, but they have been commissioned to authenticate your find. Go ahead and give them a brief synopsis of how it came about,” Matthew says.

“Well, I was lounging in my backyard one afternoon. It was so peaceful and quiet, that I was nearly going to fall asleep, but I heard a loud splash out in the water. I walked over by the seawall to see what made the noise. I looked out and saw this plastic container. I reached out and got it. When I opened it up, I found this!" Dave proudly holds up the note to show them.

Dave looks at the note. "It has instructions that say to log in to this internet site called geojamboree.com. I did just what it said, and I filled out all the information. The whole time I was thinking it was the strangest thing I have ever encountered on the river. It was fun to find that bottle. It was like an old time treasure hunt. The stuff I had to put in the website wasn't too personal, so I figured what the heck? Then, just a few days ago, I got a call from Matthew here, telling me about this trip that was set up. So, here I am. This is way cooler than I thought it would be. That's pretty much what happened. Thank you for bringing me here and paying for everything. I never thought I would ever come to London."

"Does anyone have any questions for Dave?" Matthew asks.

The group doesn't have any questions, and Dave rises from his chair to leave.

“I think they all have a handle on your story. Thank you,” Matthew says.

“You have met Dave, and his file checks out. Have you decided?” Matthew asks.

“No question, I think he is true to his word. I couldn’t pick his story apart if I tried,” John says.

Trinity, Elisabeth, and Jude all agree that Dave’s story is authentic, and they cast the unanimous vote. Matthew moves Dave’s file to the side.

“The third finder is Jimmy,” Matthew says. “He is also from the same area Dave is from, and found the bottle and the note while out doing work on the river. He is also retired and spends time doing volunteer work on the river with a local group. His background checked out fine. He logged in within the same time frame as Dave. He and Dave know each other. They had shared their stories with one another prior to today, and they were fully aware they would both be at this meeting.”

“Is it possible he copied the note from Dave?” Diane asks.

"No, that would be impossible," Matthew says. "Each note contains a unique username and password."

"Could that be easily figured out if someone knew only one of the usernames?" Diane asks.

"No, absolutely not, there isn't an obvious pattern to them and are in no way incremental in their numerical value," Matthew says. "Anyone else? If not, I will bring Jimmy in."

Jude leads Jimmy in from the richly paneled hidden door. It is so finely crafted, and blends in so well, it is hard to tell exactly where it is in the wall.

Matthew motions for Jimmy to take his seat. "I am sure you and Dave had a moment to discuss what was said in here," Matthew says.

"Yes, he told me all about it," Jimmy says.

"You are aware that this is not a judicial hearing or anything official like that. It's a private discussion to gather facts, so that this group you see here today can verify the authenticity of the note you found," Matthew says.

"Well, I am ready to answer any question you have," Jimmy says.

“Let’s start with you telling us a brief story about how you found it,” Matthew says.

“I was out checking on a logjam. You know, a logjam is a tree that falls in the river, or floats down the river from our friends in Indiana. The logjams impair the navigability of the river, so they need to come out. I was in my boat one day, looking at one, and trying to untangle some branches, when I found it. It was a sealed plastic bottle with a note inside. It took a bit to fish it out, and I darn nearly fell in the river doing it, but I got it. I opened it up, and found the note with the instructions on it. It took a few days for me to figure out the website and how to do the login, but I got it done. I thought it was some kind of media ploy, or a trick. Then, we got busy with the river cleanup, and I forgot all about it until a few days ago, when Matthew contacted me. I couldn’t believe that he was setting me up with this free all-expense paid trip to London! I thought if it turned out to be a joke, at least I had my friend, Dave, along with me.”

“There are no tricks, Jimmy, and I hope you are enjoying your stay here, with no strings attached,” Matthew says.

“Thank you, I am having fun here in London, but do you have any questions for me?” Jimmy asks.

"Do you do a lot of work on the river, Jimmy?" Jude asks.

"Oh, yes, we are on that river more often than not."

"Do you find a lot of unusual things?" Elisabeth asks.

"Besides that bottle? No, we usually just see lots of garbage and trees that fall in," Jimmy says.

Matthew thumbs through Jimmy's file for a minute. "If you don't have anything else to ask him, then we will conclude the questioning. Thank you for being here today and sharing your story with us, Jimmy," Matthew says.

"You're welcome, the pleasure is all mine. Who would have thought I would get to go to London free of charge, and with my river buddy along for the ride," Jimmy says, and he is lead out of the room.

"He sure seems like a straightforward kind of guy," Diane says.

"Yes, they both do," Trinity says. "I think they are both true to their word, and their finds are authentic."

“Are you in favor of granting his verification?” Matthew asks.

“Yes, we all agree on it,” John says.

“The fourth person is Jeff. He is from the St. Louis area, and works for an engineering firm. He found the bottle containing the note when he was out one day with his family at the Arch. His background is clean. He has no connection to any of the other finders. He logged the username in several months after the bottles were released. It appears that he has checked into the account about once every three weeks. He must really like the geojamboree website because he has over two hundred finds since the account was created. Please review his file now so I can answer your questions before he comes in,” Matthew says.

They all page through Jeff’s information, and sit back in their chairs satisfied with what they have seen. Nobody has any questions, so Jeff is lead in to the room in the same manner as the others before him. He takes his seat at the massive board room table.

“Good morning, Jeff. These are the people who will be reviewing the authenticity of the note you found. As we’ve said before to the others, this is in no way a judicial hearing. It is a private meeting to decide on the note you found. Please tell us how you found it," Matthew says.

Jeff clears his throat and starts off timidly. "It was a nice Saturday in St. Louis, and anyone who knows St. Louis knows I mean not a raging hot and humid day." He laughs.

"So my family and I went downtown to check out the sculpture festival that was going on, because we never get downtown enough, and we ended up going to the Arch. Now, I am not one who likes to go up in the Arch. If you have never been in it, it's like getting into a dryer drum. All the clanking and jumping gives me the willies, so I stayed outside until they came back down. It was a nice day, so I ended up walking out to the stairs that overlook the Mississippi River. The river was very low that day. You see, I was there during the flooding. There are about fifty stairs to the top of the Arch. During the flood, the water was all the way up to the top three stairs. I was really in awe looking at the river that day, because it was down below the seawall. There is a road between the seawall and the stairs, so you can imagine how high the river got when it flooded. I wanted to go down to the river's edge to see what it looked like from down there. It took a little time, but I walked down to the water's edge and looked back up to the stairs. Boy, it was a sight to see, knowing the water got all the way up there during that flood. I was truly amazed. I stood there for a moment, and tried to calculate how many gallons of water that must have been. I heard a boat engine behind me, and I turned around and saw a barge being pushed by a tug boat. I watched for a minute or two before something caught my eye. I looked down to see a plastic bottle floating next to the brick walkway. It was in the water, lapping up on the bricks. It was easily reachable, so I grabbed it. I dried it off the best I could, and opened it up. There was a note inside. I realized that some time had passed and my family would be coming back down from the Arch soon. I took the bottle and the note, and went back up to find them. I put the bottle in my backpack. The rest of the day was fun, and later on, when we were home, I showed my wife, Kelly, the bottle and the note. She looked at me like I made it up. I showed her the website, and that I had already logged in the username and password, and that the same note came up on the screen. She believed me after I showed her that it wasn't just a silly prank. Of course, we both thought it was the strangest thing, but since it didn't seem to be of any trouble, we didn't worry about it. Then a few weeks ago, I was at work when I got the call from Matthew about this whole trip. Our kids are grown and out of the house, and we haven't been on a vacation in a long while. I was so excited to hear that it would all be paid for, without any strings attached, so here I am."

"That was quite an impressive story about the flooding, Jeff," Matthew says.

"You seem to enjoy artistic endeavors, do you work in that sort of field?" Jude asks.

"Yes, actually I do. I take part in a lot of design planning, and I graduated from college with a major in art," Jeff says.

"Does anyone else have anything they would like to ask Jeff?" Matthew asks.

Nobody at the table has anything to ask, so Jeff is escorted out to the waiting area.

"Alright, everyone, it's been a long morning, does anyone need a break?" Matthew asks.

"Yes, I would like one," Trinity says.

"Let's take fifteen minutes, then. I will have some sandwiches and tea brought in," Matthew says, and he departs through the hidden side door. The others slowly get out of their chairs, and begin to wander around the room.

"By my count, there are still three people remaining," John says.

"So far, we have all agreed that everyone seems legitimate," Elisabeth says.

"I wonder what kinds of stories we will hear next," Diane says.

"Well, I am going to go see what is outside of this room. Anyone care to join me?" Trinity asks, and heads toward the massive set of doors they came in from.

Chapter 25 Stories

Trinity is standing at one end of the long corridor. There are many more doors lining the hall, but none are as large as the ones permitting entrance into the board room. She walks slowly, and sees there are numbers designating each room. She tries the door handle of one of them, but it is locked. She keeps walking in the direction of the elevator that they were in earlier. She doesn't remember seeing this much detail in the corridor before.

She walks past a door marked lavatory. To her relief, this door is not locked, and she boldly goes inside. As she opens the door, she is quite amazed.

"Oh, my gosh! Hey, you guys!" Trinity says. The rest of her family has caught up, and are standing behind her.

"I would never make a big deal about a restroom, but you have to see this one. It's amazing! It's like a little palace in itself," Trinity says.

The restroom was lined with the finest towels, and decorated in the finest art. The air was amazingly fresh, and they agreed that it was the most glorious anyone had ever experienced in a setting such as this.

"Look at the marble! This is just beautiful," Elisabeth says. "Now I know how good it would be to be the chief executive officer here."

"Or, the board of directors," Diane says.

"Or, us!" John says and laughs.

"Oh no," Trinity says. "I have been after you for years when we were growing up. Now, it's my turn to be first. You will have to wait your turn," Trinity says, and she closes the door.

After the break, they assemble around the board room table again. They are enjoying some sandwiches that were made exactly to their liking. The staff brings out some tea, and they watch the BBC on the ridiculously large flat panel display. Matthew slips in quietly through the paneled door and sits down at the table.

"I trust that you found all the perks we offer our guests?" Matthew asks. "When you are all ready, we can call in the next finder."

"We are all done eating, and ready to go on," Diane says. "This whole interview exercise has turned out to be a lot of fun for us."

"Yes, it's way more interesting than anything on the television," Elisabeth says.

"Bring the next person in. We are ready," John says. He grabs the remote, and shuts the entertainment system down. The screen retracts into the ceiling panel, and a door closes to hide any trace of the screen. "Impressive," John says.

"The next person is Valerie," Matthew says. "She is from New Orleans. She found the bottle and note in New Orleans, off the flood gate trail. She is a rough and tumble sort of person who is a straight talker, and has no time for dancing around subjects. She can be very blunt, but she has a good heart. Her accent is quite thick, but please do not ask her to repeat things, because she will tell you to keep your ears open, let me tell you." He laughs. "Her background checked out. She does have a few things in her past that aren't the most upstanding, but they do not impact the way she found the note. Her honesty about any background check is beyond reproach. Does anyone have any questions about her file that you have in front of you?"

"Yes, I have a question," Jude says. "There is something about an Alice in here?"

"Oh, yes," Matthew says. "That is her best friend. They grew up across the street from each other and are inseparable. They were together when they found it, but Valerie was the one who saw it first, and picked it out of the river. She will surely share any notoriety of the find with Alice."

"I see, that sounds cool to me," Jude says.

"Anyone else? Alright then, I will get her," Matthew says.

Matthew goes to open the side door, and this tall, burly woman comes in. She is wearing a pair of well pressed overalls, with a clean, white shirt underneath. She walks over to the chair, and sits down.

"Good afternoon, Valerie," Matthew says. "These people are here to listen to your experience of finding the bottle and the note. They are going to verify the legitimacy of your find. They are not within any official government capacity, and this is a private meeting."

"Well, all right," Valerie says.

"Just tell them briefly how you found the bottle and the note, and logged it into the website," Matthew says.

"Well, as you all know, I was down by the river with my best friend, Alice. We are always together. So we was down there by the locks, you know the ones that didn't help us any when that crazy lord of a storm came in, and nearly wiped N'Orleans off the map. I mean, we are a hardy city, but that ole storm sure put us into a twist! Well, anyhow, Alice and I were standing down there on that levee, and we could see the ole swamp ground out there. We was just down there to check out how it was coming back, after that nasty hurricane put a big hurt on it. Oh, it was messed up bad, and we just wanted to see it come back to the way it was. So anyway, we was down there on that levee when I saw this bottle floating along the shore. It was so close, and I thought I could reach it. So Alice says, like she always says, 'Valerie don' be going down there. If you is going to fall in, I am not taking your wet soul back in my car tonight! You would smell something awful!' and I said, come on Alice, I am quick as a rat and nimble as a possum!"

Valerie looks over to John, who has a quizzical look on his face.

"Did I say something wrong, dear?" Valerie asks.

"Well, what does a nimble possum in New Orleans look like?" John asks.

"Oh, come on son, everyone knows what a nimble possum looks like! They get into everything, and then they are gone lickity split. They are like wild voodoo spirits. Why are your ears closing up? You need to open them ears up, and hear what my story is telling you, dear!" Valerie says.

They all just look at each other and smile. None of them want to say anything, and none of them surely want to laugh out loud.

"As I was saying, I went down that levee quick as a cat, and got that bottle for Alice and I. We was plum amazed to find a note in there, and it was dry as a bone at that. That note had some strange name or user or something like that, so Alice showed me how to put it into that Internet thing. It seemed funny then, but it was no matter to us. It was a strange thing to do, but it was no stranger than all the voodoo stuff around town, so we didn't mind. Well, then this guy here calls me, and he set it all up for us to come here, and see London. Strange town, London, but kinda like N'Orleans, cause it's a lot of fun. I got to see you fine people, and everyone seems to be real nice here. Well, that's the meat of my story," Valerie says.

Matthew stands up and asks, "Anyone have any questions for her?"

They are all awestruck, and no one says a word.

"Valerie, I see you have their full attention, but I guess they don't have any questions. Thanks for coming in." Matthew leads her to the door, and she leaves the room.

"Wow! She is a firecracker, isn't she? I didn't have the guts to ask her any questions. Straight shooter isn't the word," Jude says.

"I would never question her authenticity," John says.

"So I gather everyone approves, and would vote to accept her?" Matthew asks. The group agrees. "Then, we only have two more."

"The next person is from Spain. Her name is Marta. She is a quiet person, and her English is not the greatest, but she is very astute. Her background check was the best of the whole group. She found the bottle just a few months ago. Marta is in the educational field, and I believe she is at the collegiate level of academia. As you can see from her file, she is really well rounded, and quite wise. Does anyone have any questions?" Matthew asks. They all look up at him and shake their heads no. "Alright, Jude, please bring her in."

Jude leads her into the room. "Good day, Marta. You can have a seat over here," Matthew says.

Marta slowly saunters in, and graciously sits down.

"Marta, these people are here to listen to how you found the bottle and the note. This is not an official inquisition of any kind, or related to any government activity in any way. This is a private note verification process. Do you understand?" Matthew asks.

"Yes, I understand," she says.

"Please tell them how you found the bottle with the note inside," Matthew says.

"I was out near the shore, next to the beach just outside of town. I was looking for some landscapes to photograph with my camera, and I saw this bottle floating by. I went to get it, as it was just by the shore, and it looked really interesting. After I picked it up, I saw that it had a note inside. It seemed strange to me, but I got the note out and read it. It said to go to the Internet, and fill out the form. It seemed genuine, so I went to the website. It said to wait until someone got back to me. I waited a long time, and then Matthew called me on the phone, and let me come here. He said I didn't have to pay anything, just meet with you. So, I came here, and it's so nice. I have had so much fun. I thank you or whoever is responsible for all this. This is a special adventure for me. I apologize as my English is not the best, but thank you," Marta says.

"Oh, don't worry, you are doing great," Matthew says. "Do you have anything else to add?"

"No, but do you need anything from me?" Marta asks.

"I think you did a wonderful job," Diane says. "Thanks for coming."

"Anyone else?" Matthew asks. "If no one else has anything, then let's thank Marta for her story."

They all bid Marta a good afternoon, and Matthew leads her to the paneled side door. He then returns to the table.

"She was very succinct, but I think she got her story out for you," Jude says.

"Yes, I think so," Trinity says. "I think I can speak for everyone that we are in agreement, and we approve of her story."

“Alright then, the last person is a young man named Edward. He is from Spondon, England. He just found the note a month ago. He is from Spondon, a small town not too far from here, but he has traveled the world extensively. His background checks out well. He is a very religious person, and has devoted a lot of time at his church doing everything from administrating daily functions, to running all the financials for the local diocese. He is very well educated and is a well-rounded citizen. Does anyone have any questions about his file or the information in it?” Matthew asks. They look at Matthew and shake their heads no.

“Jude, please bring Edward in,” Matthew says.

Edward strides confidently into the room, and takes a seat. He is a younger man, but looks wise for his age.

“Good day, Edward. These people are here to verify your finding of the note in the bottle. They are a neutral group, and have no stake in any notoriety of your find. They are not, in any way, here in an official government capacity. Please tell them of how you came about finding the bottle,” Matthew says.

"Let me start by saying thank you to everyone. It is a pleasure to meet you. I was on a trip to the shore, west of Spondon, to do some fishing off the docks. It's something I treasure doing every few months, and that day was perfect for it because it was quiet and calm. I was just starting to get the lures out far enough to possibly catch something when I looked down by the dock pilings. I saw a bottle bobbing out of the water. It was just out of reach, so I grabbed my fishing net and scooped it up enough to pull it up onto the dock. I wiped some of the grime off of it, and I was quite surprised that I was able to look through the clear part to see something inside. I wasn't sure if I should open it because you never know, but I grabbed a cloth to wipe it dry and I could see the piece of paper. The lid was still on tight, but I opened it up, and the note was still in great shape. It had a username and password on it, and a website to go to. So, I stowed it in my tackle box, and went about fishing. I tell you that was the best fishing day I had ever had! I caught not only the best fish, but the most fish ever. We ate like kings when I got back to Spondon. We ate so well, I completely forgot about the bottle and the note until later that evening, when I went to clean up my tackle box. There it was, just kind of beckoning to me. I went online and logged in the information. I was sure it was nothing too real, but I was game. It wasn't too long after, that Matthew called me, and set me up to come here. I thought, why not, it's only a short drive, and London is beautiful this time of year. It's not costing me anything and I was ready for a good holiday. I can honestly tell you, I have never been to Lloyd's before today. It is truly an honor to be here in this room. I will have one heck of a story when I get back home. No one will believe where I was. Even though I live on the outskirts of London, this place is a destination and a landmark for us. Thanks again for allowing me the pleasure of the visit," Edward says.

"Thank you, Edward," Matthew says. "Does anyone have any questions for him?"

"No, not me," Elisabeth says.

"Can I ask a question?" Edward asks.

"Of course," Matthew says.

"Who are all you people?"

"Well, that is Trinity, and then there is Elisabeth, Diane, John, and Jude," Matthew says.

"Let me see, are you three siblings, one brother with two sisters?" Edward asks. John, Trinity, and Diane look at each other quite taken aback.

"Yes, he is my brother and she is my sister," Trinity says.

"Elisabeth is a daughter to which one of you?" Edward asks as if he already knows the answer.

"Trinity is my mother," Elisabeth says.

"So you're all here to verify the bottle and the message inside of it. Are you here to represent the person who put the bottles out?" Edward asks.

"Yes, they are. Their mother put the bottles out quite some time ago," Matthew says.

"How long ago was it?" Edward asks.

"It was years ago," Matthew says.

"Years ago? How far did they travel then?" Edward asks.

"They traveled very far," Jude says. "They traveled all the way from Indiana. She put them in the Kankakee River."

"All the way from Indiana? That is an amazing journey! I just had to know where it came from. The majesty of finding a message in a bottle is an honor to have. It's even more special knowing it came from far away," Edward says.

"Yes, we are all amazed that one actually got to England, quite honestly," Jude says. "We figured they would be found closer to Indiana."

"Thank you for answering my questions. I am a super curious person, and this has been an adventure of a lifetime," Edward says.

"Thanks again, Edward," Matthew says.

Jude shows Edward out of the room, and takes a seat at the board room table with the others.

"He was the last one. What is your opinion of Edward?" Matthew asks.

"I am in favor, but he sure looks familiar," Jude says.

"Yes, I thought so, too," Trinity says.

"That is weird, because I was thinking the same thing," Diane says.

"Me, too," John says.

"It was like he had some connection to us," Elisabeth says. "Maybe it's just his background."

"Probably so," Trinity says.

"It sounds like you are all in agreement that his story is authentic?" Matthew asks.

They all say yes.

"That's all I have then. I would like to thank you all for coming here today. You are welcome to stay in London for a few days, with all expenses paid, before you go back home. This has been the most remarkable account I have ever taken care of. I believe you have fulfilled Ida's wishes. She must have been a truly great person. You are also welcome to tour our headquarters here. It is a wonderful piece of architecture, and there are some great works of art on display. Your badges will get you nearly anywhere in the building. It's a once in a lifetime chance, so go ahead and enjoy yourselves," Matthew says.

They all rise from their chairs and exchange handshakes and parting words. After a few minutes, they exit through the large set of doors and go out to the executive floor.

Elisabeth decides to tour all the floors, to look at every piece of art. The others look around for a few minutes, and catch their rides back to their hotels.

Elisabeth invites Trinity to take the tour with her, but she declines. She tells Elisabeth she needs to go back to the hotel to rest and relax. She has a lot to think about, and would like to rejuvenate before they go sight-seeing later. Trinity tells Elisabeth to call her when she gets back to the hotel, and she leaves her to go off on her own.

Chapter 26 Hope

Elisabeth takes her time walking around inside the building to enjoy the architecture. She has never seen anything like it, and probably will not get the chance to see it again. She stops at every point of beauty, to admire and appreciate the talent that went into each detail. Nothing has been overlooked by the artisans, and she wishes she could stay here a little longer.

Matthew departs the main board room through the paneled side door, and walks through the reception area.

"That went exceptionally well," he says to the receptionist. "Are they all still here?"

"Yes, sir, they are in the conference room down the hall," the receptionist says.

"Thanks for your assistance," Matthew says.

"You're welcome, sir."

Matthew turns down the hallway, and towards the conference room. He opens the double doors to find everyone sitting around the large table in the center of the room. His attention is diverted to the breathtaking view. The windows are immense and strategically placed to showcase the London skyline. The buildings seem to be painted in the forefront of the majestic river behind them. Matthew pauses in admiration, and gathers his thoughts before addressing the finders.

"Thank you for staying for a bit, and for your cooperation with the committee. They were very impressed with your candor and honesty. They have put in a long day with these interviews, so now they are off enjoying the sights of London. I can happily inform you that they approved the verification of all of your findings. With their approval, I am to instruct you now of the wishes of the estate. The estate set up a binding procedure to follow in order to finalize the requirements. All the conditions have been met, so I am pleased to tell you that the estate has set aside a disbursement of funds to each of you in the amount of $675,000 each. Now, I am required to disburse the funds into any form you would like, whether electronic or certified check, but the estate is not responsible for any fees or gift taxes of any kind. As such, Lloyd's will be holding out any required fees or taxes for transfer to each of your respective countries or district of citizenship. We have done enough research to take only the minimum amount required. All your expenses are still paid for, and the extra holiday spending money is included. This disbursement is on top of everything else you have been promised. I can see that you are all quite stunned at this unexpected news. Before I open the floor for questions, you need to know what to do when you leave here. It is up to you whether you discuss this with anyone or not. You can decide individually, or as a group, if you want to do a press release or a news event. Just remember to be careful about how you decide to proceed, because we all know how hungry the media is when it comes to something like this. It can take over, and have a life of its own, and leave you to wonder how you got there. The media industry is there to profit for its shareholders, so please think it over carefully. I strongly suggest taking care of your estate first. I am not soliciting you for my agency, but if you need help, we would be glad to assist you. The notes and bottles that you found are yours to keep. Please be cautious, and find a safe place for them. They could become very valuable someday. They are unique items, and will not be produced again. If I know the world we live in, they will become very rare. People from all aspects of life will seek them out. Do you have any questions?"

"Yes, I do," Edward says. "How many notes and bottles were put out?"

"All I can speak of is what the instructions said. They were clear that this meeting could not happen until at least half were found. Six constitutes half, so that makes a total of twelve bottles that were put out at the time the instructions were written," Matthew says.

"Are you saying there are at least five left out there?" Valerie asks.

"Yes, according to my instructions, there are five still remaining. They may have been found, and not logged in, or they are still out there floating around somewhere," Matthew says.

"If someone finds one of the five left, and logs it in, will they get the same disbursement as we got?" Marta asks.

"Yes, in fact, they will get the exact same amount each of you received, minus fees and taxes, of course," Matthew says with a grin.

"Let's say, for instance, if one of us finds one of those left out there, would we get another reward?" Jeff asks.

"Why, yes, you would get another disbursement of the amount you have presently," Matthews says.

"How long will the system stay in place? Until the last ones are found?" Edward asks.

“The first contract is for 75 years. That has now been partially fulfilled, so the contract begins anew, and extends for another 75 years,” Matthew says.

“Wow! This is so incredible!” Dave says. “Who put this whole thing in motion?”

“The person responsible is a woman named Ida Stone. She set up this whole adventure to be administered by her estate after her passing,” Matthew says.

“She was incredibly gifted to have created this kind of treasure hunt,” Dave says.

“Yes, I agree. It has been quite the adventure for me to administer this account, and to meet all of you. I never thought this day would come. You probably didn’t either when you found the notes and had to wait for years until I contacted you. I am sure you were as skeptical as I,” Matthew says.

Valerie shakes her head, still in disbelief. “You said a mouthful there, son,” she says.

“I have some forms that each one of you needs to fill out to formalize your disbursement. After we take care of that, you are free to roam about the building until closing time. Please enjoy the rest of your stay in London. If you need anything at all, do not hesitate to call my assistant. She can arrange for whatever you may need. It's been a long day, and quite honestly, a long couple of months, so I will be off on holiday myself to get some rest and process all that has happened. It's been the wildest time of my life, to say the least," Matthew says. He gives each of them the forms to fill out, and a Lloyd's of London ink pen.

"Oh, and keep the pen," Matthew says.

Chapter 27 Fin

In the lobby of the building, Elisabeth is looking at a beautiful piece of art, and pondering what the artist had in mind when he created it. Her mind is also busy trying to grasp the magnitude of the adventure she has had.

She can't help but remember her grandma, and all the amazing stories she told, and that her grandma has given her yet another story, even after all these years. She has been going non-stop for too many hours today, and needs to get back to the hotel to rest before she and her mom go out tonight.

She walks by the security guard and tries to hand him her security badge, but he holds his hand up and tells her to keep it as a momento of her visit to Lloyd's.

Elisabeth strolls through the porte-cochere, and waves down a taxi. When it pulls up, she opens the door to get in, and is immediately struck by the sight of someone else already in the cab.

"Oh, I am truly sorry," she says.

"No, please get in. It's me, Edward."

She relaxes, and climbs in the cab. She recognizes him now from today's interview.

"You were the last one to be interviewed," she says.

"Yes, I was. I was hoping to catch you before you left. You see, my name is Edward Stone. I have been using my research background in the information technology field to find out as much as I can about my ancestors. I have found out a lot, and I have traced some of my distant relatives back to some of your relatives. One of my relatives had left some cryptic notes about a treasure. The message described some kind of a coin of spiritual origin, and possible influence. All of my research online kept pointing to some of your accounts, and they show an increase in searches for a blessed coin. Please forgive me, but I was following your accounts and your posts, and I saw a lot of research you have been doing to verify the coin's existence. I knew I was supposed to come here to London, but I never thought you would be here, and with your family, too. I did not want to say anything in there or to anyone else, but I knew I had to catch up with you. I need you to help me search for the coin! I was hoping you knew something about it or its whereabouts."

Elisabeth is speechless. She can't believe what she is hearing. Her mind begins to race, and she can't seem to get a grip on this. It's all just too much to take in.

Edward sees a place they can speak privately, and hollers at the driver to stop. Edward takes Elisabeth by the arm, and leads her into a nearby coffee house.

"Please, Elisabeth, let's discuss this some more."

They find a secluded table in the corner, and Elisabeth starts to feel a little more relaxed.

"Well, well, my grandma did tell me a lot of stories about a coin of special power. I was also truly intrigued about its existence. I thought it must be true, because she knew so much detail about it. The problem is, is that I never found out any more about it. She passed away suddenly, and I never got to hear the whole story."

"Now what should I do, Elisabeth? I was so sure you would have some key piece of information to help me discover the legitimacy of the coin. I guess I do have time, and the means to keep searching, but I have pretty much run out of clues here and across the channel in France. Is it asking too much for you to be my guide, if I were to come to your home town to do research?"

"Oh, well, I suppose that would be alright. Yes, Edward, that would be fine. Home is a special place for me, and may possibly be of some help to you. I could show you the places my grandma told me about, but only if you promise to tell me all the family history you know. Maybe your stories can verify the truly magnificent stories my grandma told me."

"It's a deal! Thank you, Elisabeth! I promise to graciously accept your guide skills for all the knowledge I have of my ancestors!"

Made in the USA
Charleston, SC
20 May 2013